D1508221

"Without thinking about it, school age children will learn about the Civil War, not dates and boring statistics, but an insight into a soldier's life, and they will learn about the dangerous methods that were used to gather and send intelligence reports by both men and women."

—Linda Robertson, Executive Director,
Historic Manassas, Inc.

"K. E. M. Johnston has woven the perfect ghost story, packed with tension, adventure, mystery, and good ol' American History. For the middle grades, *The Witness Tree and the Shadow of the Noose* is just what the doctor ordered."

—Lois Szymanski, Author of the
Gettysburg Ghost Gang series

To Heather,
Happy Reading!

The Witness Tree and the Shadow of the Noose

Mystery, Lies, and Spies in Manassas

By
K. E. M. Johnston

W̅M̅ WHITE MANE KIDS
KIDS SHIPPENSBURG, PENNSYLVANIA

For a complete list of available publications
please write
White Mane Kids
Division of White Mane Publishing Company, Inc.
P.O. Box 708
Shippensburg, PA 17257-0708 USA

Library of Congress Cataloging-in-Publication Data

Johnston, K. E. M., 1962-
    The witness tree and the shadow of the noose : mystery, lies, and spies in Manassas / by K.E.M. Johnston.
        p. cm.
    Summary: When twelve-year-old Jake's family moves to a creepy, cramped house in historic Manassas, Virginia, on the outskirts of the famous Civil War battlefield, Jake encounters the ghost of a Confederate soldier and sets out to solve the mystery of his death.
    ISBN-13: 978-1-57249-397-1 (pbk. : alk. paper)
    ISBN-10: 1-57249-397-6 (pbk. : alk. paper)
    1. Manassas National Battlefield Park (Va.)--Fiction. [1. Manassas National Battlefield Park (Va.)--Fiction. 2. Bull Run, 2nd Battle of, Va., 1862--Fiction. 3. United States--History--Civil War, 1861-1865--Campaigns--Fiction. 4. Ghosts--Fiction. 5. Soldiers--Fiction. 6. Spies--Fiction. 7. Mystery and detective stories.] I. Title.

PZ7.J6445Wi 2009
[Fic]--dc22

                                                                2008053939

To Thomas, Wills, and James

Contents

Acknowledgments

Millions of hugs and kisses to Thomas, Wills, and James for being my harshest critics and biggest fans from the onset. Thanks to Sandy, Rochelle, Gail, Rebecca, Patti, Stephanie, Sharon, Duane, and Cathy for their priceless feedback and ceaseless enthusiasm; thanks to Susan, and thank you to Jim Burgess, museum specialist at Manassas National Battlefield Park, for his invaluable advice during the early stages.

A huge, huge thank you to my first audience, Mrs. Farouki's 2006, fifth grade class at Poplar Tree Elementary School: Walter, Peter, Rachel, Brooke, Nilima, Nikhil, Nina, Sarah, Brooke, James, Ben, Dylan, Aaron, Emily, Luke, Colby, Jessica, Sasha, Lizzet, Austin, Michael, Noah, Virginia, Hannah, Jonathan, David, and Alex.

And, of course, loving thanks to Jim.

Chapter One
Murder in Mind

In a movie, when a twelve-year-old boy hears a stranger prowling about the basement in the middle of the night, he'll summon up his courage, grab a handy dandy fire poker, and demonstrate his amazing ability as a black belt. Then he'll overpower the bad guy and save the day. But this is not a blockbuster film with a teen celebrity playing the lead. This is real. This is my life. So I did what any other self-respecting kid would do. I hid my head under my pillow and prayed for a miracle.

Then the sound echoed again. Heavy, ominous thuds of size thirteen feet dragging along a cement basement floor.

"Come on, Jake, come on," I said to myself, peeking out from under the pillow. "You're a sixth-grader in middle school. You listen to unedited rap. How can you be scared?" When my eyes adjusted to the half-light, I noticed a shadow reflected on my closet door of a hangman's noose and a body, its head twisted at an impossible right angle. Screaming eyes bulged out of a skeletal face. The corpse swayed rhythmically to and fro as it dangled in the night breeze. A gnarled bough of the old oak tree in the front yard creaked in an effort to support its weight.

Small hairs tingled on the back of my neck while goose bumps peppered my skin. It's a trick of the moonlight shining through our bedroom window causing a shadow, I reasoned. There's no dead body. Ha ha. Stupid. I tried to laugh but a loud crash downstairs caused my heart to pound so hard I thought it might explode into tiny fragments at any second and come flying out of my mouth.

I looked over at Danny, my eight-year-old brother, sleeping like a baby, oblivious to the intruder in our house. Tonight, even the familiar squeak, squeak, squeak of Raffles, my pet hamster, running the marathon on its wheel at the end of my bed, failed to distract my terror.

This was not the first time I had heard the intruder. Whenever I complained to Mom, she said I was imagining it. But I wasn't. The noises were real, and the day my parents believed me would be the day they found my dead body.

This was no good. I could not lie in bed any longer waiting like a helpless prey caught in a trap. Someone had to go down and confront the intruder.

Danny.

I grabbed a flashlight from the drawer next to my bed and sneaked over to wake my brother. The time had come to cross the line. Literally.

In between our two beds, I had duct-taped a partition-line on the carpet. And for a very good reason. My brother is not your typical eight-year-old. He's way too smart for his age, and his obsession with the American Civil War is kind of disturbing. He sleeps in a Confederate uniform and a gray infantry hat, called a kepi—he goes mad if you get the terminology wrong. The walls on his side of the room are plastered with Civil War reenactment posters, and under his pillow rests a replica sword that he'd picked up at a yard sale last summer. He almost speared himself in his excitement. But he has his uses, and tonight he would serve as my bodyguard.

Hopping over discarded T-shirts and dirty jeans, my flashlight caught Danny's Civil War magazines standing neatly at attention under his bed like the graves at Arlington National Cemetery. He'd spent the past evening sorting them in date order.

"Danny, Danny," I murmured close to his ear. "Wake up."

He opened his eyes a crack. "We're not allowed out of bed until seven," he grunted.

Danny was a rule follower.

"He's back," I whispered, trying to control the tremble in my voice.

Danny opened his eyes wide and shook his head with the ferocity of a wolf shaking its kill. "Go away."

"I'll pay you," I said. "Two dollars."

"Ten."

Danny was also a very rich eight-year-old.

"Fine. Ten dollars. Bring your sword," I said.

Danny dragged his small body out of the warm bedclothes. "It's not very sharp."

"I know that, but the guy in the basement doesn't. Just be real quiet. We don't want to wake Mom and Dad."

"Can Edward come too?" Danny whispered as he slipped his small feet into his brown, plaid slippers. Edward was Danny's invisible friend. He'd joined the family the day after we moved. Mom had said that even though we'd only moved a couple of blocks to a smaller house, it was still traumatic for Danny. Danny didn't like change.

"No," I said. "Leave him here. He'll be safer in the bed-room." I didn't want Danny tripping over Edward if we had to make a quick getaway.

Out in the hallway we tiptoed past our parents' room. Dad's snoring sounded like a snowplow with faulty ignition. At the top of the stairs, Danny raised his right arm up in the air.

"What are you doing?" I hissed.

"I'm preparing to fight. Stonewall Jackson always held up his hand when he rode into battle."

"Why?" I asked nervously.

"Because he thought one side of his body was bigger than the other."

Okay.

A thought occurred to me. "Didn't Stonewall Jackson get killed?" I said.

"Yes," Danny replied, still holding his arm up in the air. "He was shot by his own men."

Great.

"Come on," I said, my palms sticky with sweat. "And don't make a sound."

Downstairs a full moon, shining through the glass of the front door, lit up the hallway as it reflected off the five inches of snow lying on the ground. As we crept toward the basement, we heard the sound of someone stomping up and down in rage coming from underneath our feet. I stopped dead.

"Did you hear that?" I whispered.

"Yes," said Danny. "Are we going to die?"

Almost definitely.

I gripped my brother by the shoulders, and looked him straight in the eyes. "No." I gulped and it felt like a large lump of fresh bread had wedged in my throat.

Danny's face paled as white as the snow outside. "I think we should get Mom." He turned to go back upstairs.

"Wait, Danny," I said, holding him firmly by the arm. "The last time Mom looked when I heard a noise, there was no one there, and she thought I was making it up. This time we're going to show her how smart we are. We're going to find some proof. She'll be really proud of her soldiers."

Little kids love making their mom proud. I knew I was on to a winner.

Reluctantly Danny agreed and very carefully we opened the door to the basement. The shaft from the flashlight pointed down the steps like a light saber. I pushed Danny ahead of me. I was many things, but I was not brave.

"You go first. Your footsteps won't make so much noise," I said.

He believed me, and slower than slugs in the afternoon sun we inched down to face the enemy.

Our basement was a pretty standard scary basement. The realtor had described the house as historic. In my word list, historic meant run down or dilapidated (last week's new vocabulary word). My parents had claimed the house had been a bargain.

"I can't believe we got such a steal," Mom had said. "We would never have been able to afford this otherwise. Mrs. Snell certainly seemed in a hurry to leave."

"That old woman was a lunatic," Dad had laughed.

The house was falling down and creepy. That's why it was so cheap. Naturally no one wanted to hear my opinion. But at least we didn't have to change schools.

The basement had a back door and a window, making it slightly less eerie. But it crawled with crickets and hairy spiders up in the rafters that entertained themselves by dripping into your hair. Old scraps of carpet obscured the concrete floor and the whole room smelled worse than the boys' bathrooms at school. Mom said it was cats.

She'd never been in our bathrooms.

At the far end of the room a door with a shiny gold knob led into a small storage area. We could hear someone pacing up and down behind the door.

"Lock him in," suggested Danny, tugging my sleeve and pointing to the bolt at the top of the door jam.

Gingerly, I reached up and tried to slide the old, rusty lock, but it wouldn't budge. I shrugged, exasperated. What now?

The noise stopped abruptly, and I heard a gasp. An icy breeze swept across my forehead as the temperature in the basement dipped.

"Hurry up," Danny mouthed, his eyes wide and his pupils dilated.

I could barely grip the lock, my hands were shaking so much. "It's stuck," I said.

Suddenly the doorknob started to turn. He was coming out! I took a deep breath, and with strength I didn't even know I had, I forced the bolt with both hands. With a start it snapped into place.

"Quick," I yelled to Danny. "Run!"

We tore upstairs like two deer fleeing a hunter and hammered on Mom's bedroom door, bursting in without waiting for an answer.

Mom hushed us out of the room and closed the door gently behind her, her face flamed in anger. "I've had enough of this, Jake. I can't believe you woke up your little brother. You almost disturbed your dad, too, and he has an interview tomorrow."

"Mom, we *both* heard him," I challenged. "The guy's in the storage room. I don't know what he wants, but we locked him in. This time you can definitely call the cops."

"I am *not* calling the police again." Mom ushered us down the stairs. "They were here three days ago and they warned you about making hoax claims. We'll get a fine and I'll get into serious trouble. Are you quite certain you both heard something?" She looked specifically at Danny.

We nodded vigorously.

"It's probably a trapped animal like a skunk or a raccoon," she reasoned.

Then it should be in the circus if it can turn a doorknob, I thought, but said nothing.

"I'll go and have another look," she sighed. "But this is absolutely, positively the last time. Danny, bring your sword." She smiled slightly as Danny proudly led the way. She wasn't a bad mother.

"What about Edward?" asked Danny.

Mom yawned. "If he's awake, then he can come too."

We hurried down to the basement where Mom also struggled with the lock. Eventually she managed to yank it back and opened up the storage room door. I snapped on the light.

Nothing. Zip. Nada. Zilch. No animal, vegetable or mineral revealed itself. Cardboard boxes lined the shelves.

"Search around the floor," said Mom. "See if you can spot any animal droppings."

We peered under the shelving and in the corners. Only boxes. No sign of poop. No murderer's footprints.

"Right, Jake." Mom's voice was firmer now. "I'm sorry to spoil your little game, but enough is enough. Look around. No living thing has been here, so I do not want to hear any more on this subject. Do you understand?"

"Yes," I said in a sullen voice.

We walked back through the basement, and I glanced outside, through the glass pane in the door, at the white blanket of snow. Then, out of the corner of my eye, I saw it. An outline of a figure flew across the lawn. I peered harder, trying to focus as Mom came up behind me. The hairs on my arms stood up and my skin felt all prickly. I tried to control my breathing.

"Did you see that?" I whispered.

"What now?" Mom stood next to me, her hand on her hip as she peeked out into the backyard.

"I saw something. A shape," I said.

"Jake," she said. "If someone was out there, don't you think they would have left footprints in the snow?"

The ground was as untouched as a pre-game baseball pitching mound.

Chapter Two

Stranger Than Fiction

At the end of the afternoon at school the following day, I gave my friend, Raj Gupta, a rundown of my latest brush with death. My head was buried in my locker as I searched for a mislaid history book. The clock was ticking. We had a measly three minutes between classes to get a drink, go to the bathroom, and get our stuff from our locker. A bit of extra stress between lessons, just what every sixth-grader needs.

"He was definitely there again, Raj." My voice echoed inside the metal cabinet. "I'm convinced he's hiding in the house but I've no idea how he manages to escape through locked doors. It's really creepy."

Raj strained to hear as the entire school crushed around us. The lockers stood in the center hall of Longstreet Middle School. On the surrounding walls three-foot murals of Harriet Tubman, Abraham Lincoln, and Martin Luther King, Junior, looked on. Every available free space in the school screamed excellence, success, and perseverance like grand prizes there for the taking. But as the paper missiles flew overhead in a steady stream, and you watched your back constantly in case of an attack from a disgruntled eighth-grader, you had to wonder.

"Tell me after Social Studies," said Raj. "We need to hurry. I don't want to be late for history."

Raj was never late for anything. We were complete opposites, but we'd been friends since second grade and I'd hung on to him like I would a pair of favorite sneakers.

Finally I located my text book, and keeping our time in the danger zone to a minimum, we sprinted over to our last period.

We were covering American Civil War spies, and it was so boring. Social Studies was my least favorite subject. And because my mom was the curator at the nearby Manassas National Battlefield Park, the teacher, Ms. Browne, with an 'e,' seemed to think she and I had some kind of connection. She reminded me constantly how fortunate I was to be living in Northern Virginia where the major battles of the Civil War took place. But history, for me, was about as exciting as going to the dentist on a warm, sunny afternoon when everyone else was outside shooting hoops. She had the enthusiasm of a pack of cub scouts at a national s'mores convention, couldn't get enough of the Underground Railroad (which was not the Washington, DC, Metro, I found out a few weeks ago), and could go on for hours about stone walls and declarations.

She also had the dress sense of a blind two-year-old. Today she was wearing around her neck a red band supporting a hefty iron cross about two inches long. She looked like a Goth crossed with a librarian, and if she made a sudden move, she'd get a black eye, for sure.

"In the Cold War, Ethel Rosenberg was executed for being a spy," Ms. Browne said to the sea of blank faces. "Who can tell me why that would *not* have happened during the Civil War?"

No one spoke. I stifled a yawn. This was a tough question. Ms. Browne turned to Alan Idle, our resident class clown. Alan was as tall as an NBA basketball player with the build of a football linebacker. With his squinty eyes that dissolved into the folds of his face, he was not someone you'd want to meet in an alley after dark. He was not someone you'd want to meet, period.

"Alan, could you tell me why Ethel Rosenberg would not have been executed for spying in the Civil War?"

Alan peered down at his textbook, then back up at the class and grinned.

"Because she wasn't born yet?" he said in his squeaky, girly voice. He sounded like he'd swallowed a mouthful from a helium balloon. His voice did not go with his build. A couple of kids snickered in the back of the classroom.

"No, Alan," said Ms. Browne in a stern voice. "That was not the answer I was looking for. Who can tell Alan the real reason? Come on, someone take a guess."

Raj stuck up his hand.

"Yes, Raj?" said Ms. Browne.

Raj glanced over at Alan, thereby signing his own death warrant. No one likes a smart-brain. "Because she was a woman," he said in a loud, crisp voice.

The class erupted in laughter. Alan Idle cackled the loudest.

But Ms. Browne smiled sweetly. "That is correct, Raj. Although any *man* caught spying in the Civil War would be immediately hanged on the nearest tree," she went on, "in the eighteen-sixties the American army did not think it proper for a lady to swing from the gallows. Although women spies were not completely immune from capital punishment, many times they were simply reprimanded, then allowed back to their homes, where they would be free to spy again."

I sneaked a quick peek at Alan. He was drumming his fingers on his desk in the same way a bull paws the ground with his hoof before it charges. Raj saw this too and his big brown eyes opened wide in dismay.

As soon as the bell rang, Raj and I made a run for the door, but Alan caught up with us in the hallway.

"You can get lost," he said to a couple of kids hanging around. They didn't need written instructions and fled immediately. Alan grabbed Raj by the arm and twisted it behind his back. "Think it's clever to make me look like an idiot, do you, butt-head?"

"You don't need my help," Raj winced, attempting to hide the pain of having his arm ripped out of its socket. "You manage that perfectly well by yourself."

Not what I would have said.

"You and me are going to take a little walk." Alan pushed Raj down the hall. I trailed behind, unsure what to do. Alan Idle was almost twice my weight and height.

"It's you and I," Raj corrected.

I groaned, hiding my face in my hands as Alan steered Raj toward his locker. I looked around for a teacher, but they were never around when you needed them. Still holding Raj firm, Alan grabbed a can of deodorant out of his locker and pointed it at Raj's face. Alan sprayed, then lifted his knee into a very delicate area. Raj crumpled like a retreating Jack-in-the-box. I stepped forward to help Raj as Tiger *Cool Kid* Stone appeared.

In his cut-off vest and baggy jeans, all four feet ten inches of Tiger screamed cool. And with his blond movie-star hair, which had to take a pot of hair gel a week, he walked the walk and talked the talk.

"Is this guy bothering you, dude?" Tiger said to Raj. Despite his size Tiger had the confidence of a freshly appointed bus patrol.

I had no clue why Tiger Stone was coming to the rescue, but this wasn't the time for twenty questions. For a second, I could feel the tension between Tiger and Alan like two dogs guarding their own territory.

In the food chain, Tiger Stone was the deadly hawk and Alan Idle the field mouse. Raj and I weighed in with the grasshoppers.

Alan backed off. "Another time," he rasped gravely, then stomped away.

"Thanks," Raj muttered to Tiger.

Tiger draped a muscular arm that could rival Popeye's around Raj's shoulders. "You and me are buddies, and that's what you do for buddies." He coughed and paused for a second. "So, about the big test tomorrow?"

"The Math review?" said Raj hesitantly.

"Yes. You see, the thing is," Tiger gave an exaggerated sniff, "I figured, it would be advantageous to all parties, if," he hesitated for effect, "I sat next to you during the test. You know what I'm saying?"

He wanted Raj to cheat!

"What if we get caught?" said Raj.

Tiger threw a sympathetic glance my way. "Raj. Raj, you're embarrassing me. I'm not asking you to cheat. What kind of a kid do you think I am? I know all the stuff. I've been revising for weeks, I just haven't had a chance to refresh, that's all." He sounded as phony as the salesman who'd tried to sell Mom a new car last week.

"And I just need to sit next to you," repeated Raj, avoiding my eyes.

"That's all." Tiger turned to go. "You're cool, man," he called over his shoulder as he waltzed away.

"What are you doing?" I screamed at Raj when Tiger Stone was out of earshot. "Are you crazy? Tiger Stone is way more trouble than Alan Idle. At least with Alan you know what you're up against, a couple of whacks and he's done. Tiger Stone is pure evil. You know who he is? His two older brothers are in the Skull gang. You do *not* want to mess with the Stone kids."

"Yes, but Tiger Stone is Alan Idle's enemy," Raj said. "And your enemy's enemy has to be your friend."

Raj said some strange things sometimes.

"I didn't do the right thing, though, did I?" Raj said in a gloomy voice, as we stepped out of the stuffy school building into the chilly afternoon air. "I should have said no to Tiger Stone. Dadaji says, 'He who rides the tiger can never dismount.'"

Dadaji was Raj's granddad, and Raj just loved his proverbs.

Outside, I looked up at the large sign with Longstreet Middle School painted in large gold letters on it. Underneath the name the school always posted a message like details of upcoming band concerts, or picture day, or the "welcome back students we love you" lies. That afternoon, the sign voiced new words of wisdom. To celebrate Martin Luther King, Junior's birthday, the board displayed one of his statements: *The Time Is Always Right To Do What Is Right.*

"Don't look at the sign," I said. "Close your eyes."

We did and promptly collided.

As we headed home, we were both very quiet, lost in our own troubles. Finally, Raj brought up the subject of the intruder.

"Do you really believe there's someone hiding in your basement?" Raj asked when we were almost at my house.

"Yes. I'm positive of it. The strange thing is I only ever hear him at night. If you want to know the truth, Raj, I'm scared to death. What if he decides to come upstairs? What am I going to do? Without any proof, Mom won't believe there's anyone there."

"What about your dad? What does he say?"

"He laughs and says it's a ghost." I scuffed my feet against a low brick wall.

"Really?" Raj's face showed his surprise.

"Yeah, but he's just messing with me. He thinks the whole thing is hilarious. No one, except Danny, believes me."

"Well, my advice is to keep out of his way. The prowler I mean, not your dad. You can keep ten yards from a horse, and a hundred yards from an elephant, but the distance you should keep from a wicked man cannot be measured."

"Is that another one of your granddad's dumb proverbs?" I asked.

"Yeah," said Raj, flashing his white teeth in a wry smile.

"But I can't keep away, Raj," I said. "I have to find out what he wants. I have to find out if we're in danger."

Chapter Three

Enemies for Friends

After dinner that night, Danny and I were hanging out in our bedroom. I still had a ton of homework to do, and I stared dismally at the mountain of papers in front of me. I booted up the computer and clicked on to Instant Messaging, but none of my friends were online.

Just as I was about to get started, my US history book, stuffed with loose papers, clattered from the pile on my desk to the floor. It was kind of weird, like it had jumped all by itself.

But then my desk *was* crowded. A slight knock would have easily dislodged a book. I needed a bigger desk. I needed a bigger bedroom. There wasn't enough space to swing a yo-yo. I rescued the book, which had opened on the page about Civil War spies, *boring*, and wedged it back on my desk between my *Life Science* book and the computer screen.

Danny was busy searching all the crevices in his bed for money. It seemed, for the second night running, the tooth fairy had ignored the molar under Danny's pillow.

"It's your sword," I pointed out. "She's petrified she's going to rip off her wings if she comes anywhere near your head."

"Maybe she put the money under *your* pillow?" he said hopefully.

"Maybe you should tell Mom instead of keeping it a big secret. She does have a direct line to the fairy world, you know."

"I don't believe you." Danny launched himself onto my quilt.

I turned back to my books to make some sense of pre-algebra when I noticed frantic scratching coming from my hamster's cage. Something appeared to be upsetting him.

Now Raffles is a fairly large hamster. If they had Sumo wrestling for mammals he'd flatten any contestant within five seconds. Let's say he's not exactly nimble on his feet. But today, instead of squatting like a deflated basketball in his favorite corner of the cage, like he usually does during daylight hours, he was spinning around and around, emitting a piercing squeak, like he was in terrible pain. I looked over into his cage.

"Danny!" I gasped. "Why did you put a headless toy soldier in my hamster's cage? And is that ketchup on his jacket, or real blood?"

"It wasn't me," said Danny, clambering off my bed and peering in.

"If you didn't put the toy in there, then who did?" I asked, poking my fingers between the bars of the cage as I tried to stroke Raffles' smooth albino fur.

"It's Ulysses Grant!" wailed Danny, opening the cage and snatching his headless general before hopping back onto my bed.

Raffles, usually a friendly creature, raised himself up onto his hind legs, then sunk his little sharp teeth into my flesh. I let out a yelp, and Mom, still in her green park service uniform and smelling like our flower patch in the summer, stepped in the room.

"What's the matter, honey?"

I stared down at my finger. "Raffles bit me because Danny reenacted a Civil War skirmish on Hamster Hill. Now he won't let me near him. He's running all over his cage like he's on fire."

"It wasn't me," insisted Danny.

"Look, he's scared stiff." I noticed a pile of fur in the corner. "And he's going bald." I leaned down and placed my head close to his cage. "Hey, Pal, it's okay."

Raffles stopped racing around and cowered in the corner, his crimson eyes like drops of blood in the snow. Then, a strange sensation came over me. I felt like there was someone else in the room. Goose bumps returned to my skin, and reflected in the mirror in the corner of Raffles' cage, I saw a man standing behind me. He had a scar above his eye. I whirled around. But there was nobody there.

"Where's he gone?" I said.

"Who, honey?" asked Mom.

"There was a man. Standing right there. He had a scar and—"

Mom clicked her tongue impatiently. "Not again, Jake, and watch out, you're dripping blood on the carpet."

There's nothing like sympathy from a loved one.

Had I imagined him?

"Let me see your finger," Mom said.

I held it out.

"It's just a little prick. You'll live. Keep an eye on it, and let me know if it starts to hurt."

Danny returned to rooting about under my sheets.

"What are you up to, Danny?" Mom asked.

"Nothing," he said, sitting up straight in the middle of my bed.

Mom's eyebrows headed to the ceiling but she didn't say a word. At this rate, Danny had more chance of playing in the NBA than he did of getting his tooth money. Parents and tooth fairies had an unspoken agreement. Fool one and you fool them all.

I turned back to my homework, and stared at my computer. It had reverted to standby mode, and a bloody image of a battle filled the screen.

"Danny, would you quit changing the screensaver," I snapped.

"It wasn't me," Danny said from the bed.

I felt a hand on my shoulder and my history book took a nosedive again. I whipped around and glanced down. For the second time the book had fallen open at the chapter on Civil War spies, and a Civil War nurse in an old, grainy photograph stared up at me. I felt a shiver run through me and I peered around the room. What was in here? What unexplained force had placed a Union general in my innocent hamster's cage and kept hurling my Social Studies textbook to the ground? I picked up the book, shoved it to the back of my desk, and shook my head. I couldn't think about it now. I had a big test the next day, and needed to tackle the strange and curious world of quadrilaterals and parallelograms.

Mom went back downstairs, and Danny sneaked up behind me. He tugged at my sleeve. I leaped a mile into the air.

"Jeez, Danny, don't creep up on me like that," I said.

"Look what I found under your pillow." He held a green ticket stub an inch from my nose. "When did you go to the Battlefield Park, and why didn't you take me?"

I had no clue what he was talking about. I took the ticket and turned it over in my fingers. *Admit One, Manassas National Battlefield Park.* On the reverse was a drawing in blood-red of what looked like an upside down anchor.

"I've never seen it before," I said. "Anyway, why would I buy a ticket to where Mom works? We get in for free."

Danny stared at the sketch on the back of the ticket. "That looks like a drawing of the red ribbon the nurses wore during the Civil War."

I studied the ticket closer. "But why would anyone sketch that? Do you think it's some kind of message?"

"You mean from the tooth fairy?" asked Danny hopefully.

I laughed to hide my concern. "Yeah, the tooth fairy." Who else could it be?

"Can I keep it?" Danny asked.

"Sure." I flicked the ticket back to him. "Now go away so I can finish my studying."

Two hours later, I lost the power of sight.

I was in the shower, in the middle of washing my hair, when everything went dark. I started to panic.

"Mom? Anybody?" I yelled. "Help. I've gone blind."

Mom's voice came through from the other side of the bathroom door. "You haven't gone blind, Jake. There's been an outage, that's all. I expect it's because of the snowstorm. There's so much ice sitting on the wires outside it has brought down some of the power lines. Turn off the water and dry yourself, then come out to your bedroom. And be careful not to slip. I'm going to go and find the flashlights." I could hear Mom muttering to Danny as her voice slipped away.

It's very strange showering in pitch black. Not bad strange, just peculiar strange. Reaching out for the faucet I turned off the water, then held my hands out in front of me and touched the cool tile on the shower walls. As I felt my way around to the towel rack, I heard a tapping coming from the other side of the door. Then someone tried the door handle.

"Mom, is that you?" I cried.

Then, like a runaway snowboard, it hit me. This was the work of the stranger in the basement. It was a setup. I was willing to bet my little brother's savings that we were the only house without power. The crazy guy had severed the lines. He'd probably cut the telephone wire too. This was all in his master plan.

Danny's torso would be dumped on his bed—his dismembered head impaled on one of his Civil War bayonets— it's what Danny would have wanted at least. Danny's guts would have been carelessly tossed about the room. I could picture the blood trickling down his poster of the Second Battle of Bull Run. The carpet would be ruined. Mom would be furious. Dad would have survived, sprawled out comatose on the downstairs sofa in front of the TV. And the shadowy figure would finally come to claim me as his ultimate victim in a long string of gruesome murders.

Oh sure, Mom would try to stop him, bravely putting herself between him and her two dear sons. But her mind would wander as it frequently does. You know when your mother tells you she's listening but you can tell by her glazed expression that she's thinking about your missing library book or the stain on the living room rug. Today, Mom would have remembered the carrot cake baking in the oven.

The tapping resumed at the door. Was he using the severed finger of my precious younger brother? What did he want from me? I was no use to him.

But I couldn't stay in the bathroom forever. I seized the toilet plunger and prepared to confront the demon.

Chapter Four

A Stranger Revealed

"What do you want?" I hissed, my voice shaking.

"I need to pee," said a small voice. "Hurry up."

I unlocked the door and opened it a crack. A small hand appeared on the frame.

"Jake, I really gotta go." Danny leaped in and tried to elbow me out the room. I placed my hands either side of his face, pinched his cheeks, and kissed his forehead.

"Get off," he yelled. "I can't wait. I'm gonna wet my pants. And leave the door open. I'm scared."

I smiled with relief at my brother and embraced the walls of the dark hallway as I slipped into our bedroom and walked over to the window. Mom had been right, of course. The lamp outside my window was as useful as a candle at the bottom of the sea. All the homes in the neighborhood were in darkness, with the snow on the ground offering a dim glow as the yards and the streets converted to nightlights. Discarded orange and yellow plastic snow saucers peppered the snow with bursts of color, and fresh snow filled the crevasses left by our sledding.

Then I heard the unmistakable clumsy tread on the stairs, and froze paralyzed with fear.

"Mom? Dad?" I called in a low whisper, edging toward the side of my bed, unable to shake the image of the murderer creeping toward my room ready to pounce in the darkness, sharp knife at the ready.

"It's just me, honey," called Mom. "Your dad's still out. I'll be there in a minute."

I lay back and waited as my eyes grew accustomed to the dimness. Unidentified shapes lurked in every corner.

Then the strangest thing happened. The shadow of the noose reappeared very distinct against the grey of my closet door. But there was no means of light to cause the shadow. Yet it was a definite shadow. And when I stretched out my arm to break it, the shadow remained intact. But you can't have a shadow without light. It's not possible. A wave of icy fear swept through me as my brother stumbled into the room.

"Danny," I said. "Can you see the hangman's noose?"

But before Danny could register what I was saying, it faded and disappeared.

Was it a trick of the light, again?

Beams of light marched through our open door as if hunting for fugitives. Mom had returned.

"Here, I brought flashlights," she said. "What's the matter, Jake? You look like you've seen a ghost."

"I'm fine," I said, pulling a sweater over my head.

Danny cartwheeled onto his bed and collapsed into the shape of a starfish. "Is Jake going crazy like Uncle John?"

"No, of course not," said Mom, standing by the door. "And there's no point getting dressed, Jake. You might as well get to sleep, both of you. I don't expect the power will be back on until morning."

Mom left us each with a flashlight and a plate of cookies, and I started to wonder. Was Danny right? Was I going nuts like Uncle John? Would I start roaming off in the middle of the night and forget who I was and where I was going?

What other explanation could there be? Bad guys don't hide in basements and escape through locked doors. How come I heard footsteps in an empty room and felt drastic changes in temperature? Why did I see deathly shadows, like someone was in the room with me, breathing over my face, weighing on me like an unexplained presence?

Unless...

My heart thumped like a jackhammer as I felt a cold wind brush against my bare ankles when I pulled back the sheets on my bed. I watched horrified as a feathery shadow flitted across my bed and over to the window. It was not my imagination. I was sure of it, and climbing into bed, shaking like Jell-O, I noticed a crumpled up piece of paper on the ground. In the beam of my flashlight, I could see the faded yellow of parchment and I leaned over and picked it up. It looked about two hundred years old and appeared to be a part of a letter. Most of the words were smudged, but I could just make out some of the words.

"Danny, look what I found on the ground."

I read aloud: *August 28, 1862—Longstreet regiment moving eastwards through White Plains—Jackson right flank intended—*

"1862 was the battle of Manassas," piped up Danny in an excited tone. How could he be so joyful, when I was four years older and scared stiff?

The possibility that I had just witnessed a ghost seemed too ridiculous to even consider. I mean, come on! Seeing a ghost is not exactly something you're open to in sixth grade. Ghosts, ha? They're not real. They're right up there with fairies and goblins and monsters in the closet.

But the more I thought about it, the more it made sense and yet no sense. Startled pets playing with headless toy generals. Tickets we hadn't bought, with weird drawings on the back, to museums we could go to for free. The absence of footprints in the snow. Secret notes.

I could not ignore the evidence any longer. We had a ghost. A real live—well dead—Civil War ghost was cohabiting with the Salmon family. *Tight*.

Right?

Chapter Five

Things That Go Bump in the Night

The following morning, Danny and I were at the kitchen table stuffing our mouths with sugared cereal. I'd hardly slept the night before as I listened intently for the ghost to return. My guess is I had two hours sleep filled with dreams about dismembered ghouls and headless horsemen.

Why was the ghost here, in my house, and why now? The noises had started last Saturday night. I remembered because during the day, Dad had been injured with the new gas-powered chainsaw he'd got for Christmas. He'd said that now he had time on his hands he was going to tidy up the backyard. And after felling everything above mushroom height, he'd turned to the front yard intending to chop down the old oak tree. Mom and I were dead set against it. We loved that tree with its branches like bony fingers of a shrewd old wizard concocting a particularly gruesome spell. Mom had said it was a white oak and was probably around during the Civil War. She also said that the old trees were referred to as "witness trees." But it seemed Dad loved his chainsaw more.

"The tree is way too big, Jake. We get no sunlight on the front of the house. I'll plant a nice flowering cherry in its place. You'll love it," he'd said.

Did I look like a flowering cherry kinda kid?

I had been shooting hoops in the driveway as the chainsaw raged into action. But as the glint of afternoon sun on the metal casing caught my eye, I had looked over in horror to see the silver blades dislocate one by one from the machine and fly out as if being fired by an invisible knife thrower. They had stabbed Dad multiple times in the arm, causing patches of bright red to spread out on the fabric of his sweatshirt like ink spills on a white tablecloth.

"Jake, get your mother, quick!"

Mom had come running out and had reassured us that it was just a surface graze, and Dad had lost interest in the chainsaw and disappeared inside to nurse his wounds. Our tree had lived to see another day.

In bed, later that night, as I'd looked out at the oak looming tall against the night sky with its peeling bark worse than my acne, I knew if it could survive a Civil War, it could certainly survive my dad. That night was when the unexplained noises in the basement had begun.

Was there some connection between the tree and the ghost? Had there been a battle right here in our yard with our witness tree smack in the middle? If I concentrated really hard, I swear I could smell the gunpowder from the cannons and imagine the blood seeping from the dead soldiers into the wet mud as the armies from the North and the South blasted each other to pieces. Maybe Dad attacking the tree had brought the ghost out of its grave.

Mom's urgent voice brought me back to the present. "Danny, have you been eating the lemons again? I need one for dinner tonight and there are none in the fruit bowl."

I glanced at Danny. "Nobody eats lemons. It's not normal," I said, taking a swig of my orange juice.

"Stonewall Jackson loved lemons. He sucked them before every battle," Danny said. He had his Civil War book propped open with his elbow. "Did you know one million horses died during the Civil War? That's over three times as many as men." His little eyes darted across the pages of the book. "Guess what General Meade's horse was called."

"Surprise me," I said.

"Baldy." Danny snickered.

The thing with Danny was he sucked you in. You had no interest in Civil War trivia, but you just had to ask. "Didn't he have any hair?" I said.

"Of course he did. But they boiled horses' hair to sew up the soldiers' wounds."

You learned more history in five minutes with Danny than two hours with Ms. Browne, with an 'e.' I peered over at Danny's book. "Are you reading about Civil War horses or something?"

"How did you know?" Danny asked, revealing the title.

"Lucky guess," I shrugged.

Mom disappeared for a second into the laundry room, returning laden with our backpacks. "Hurry up, boys. You're going to be late for school. Are you buying lunch today or do you want me to pack?"

"What is it?" I asked.

"Pizza. It's always pizza on Fridays," said Mom.

"I'll buy," I said. School pizza was about as tasty as microwaved cardboard. But pizza was pizza.

"Me, too," said Danny.

"Make sure you eat the fruit too," said Mom, who could never get enough of her food groups.

Danny's nose went back in his book, and I scooped up the last of my cereal, then turned to my brother.

"Danny?" I said.

He didn't answer. He was lost in *The Mutinous Mules at Brandy Station.*

I shook his arm and frosted flakes catapulted into the air. "Do you believe in ghosts?" I used a low voice so that Mom wouldn't hear.

Danny studied his empty spoon for a second, then yelled, "Mom, Jake made me spill my cereal."

"Don't be such a baby," I said and rephrased the question. "Do you think ghosts exist?"

"Sure," he said, shoveling another spoonful of flakes into his mouth.

"Well, I think the noises in the basement are made by a ghost." I remembered the flying chainsaw blades. "An angry one."

"Jake!" barked Mom with her back to me at the kitchen sink. She spoke not in a "have a nice day" tone, but more of a "what have I told you" voice. My mother had better hearing than a bat. That worried me sometimes.

"Maybe it's the ghost of the old woman who used to live here," Danny suggested, ignoring Mom's frown.

"I don't think she died," I said, pushing my empty cereal bowl to the side. But Danny had raised a good point. Maybe the old lady knew something about the ghost. "Mom, didn't you say the old lady agreed to sell this house at a really low price, like she couldn't wait to leave?"

"I may have said that," said Mom carefully, picking up our breakfast dishes and rinsing them under running water. "But that doesn't mean she saw a ghost. I'm sure she had perfectly good reasons to sell. Now go and brush your teeth and forget this nonsense."

I decided to talk to Raj. We'd only just moved into this neighborhood, but Raj had lived in this town in the same house since he was born. I was sure he'd be able to tell us something about the previous owner of our home.

At my first opportunity at school the next day, I located Raj. He was standing in the hall outside the boys' toilets nursing a bloody nose.

"I thought you were getting protection from your new buddy, Tiger Stone?" I said.

"I decided not to help Tiger in the test. But that was clearly a bad idea." The tissue he was holding had turned bright scarlet. "Alan was pissed because I stepped on his shoe."

"You could tell a teacher," I suggested, but without conviction. We knew the rules. Being a tattletale does not help. Not in sixth grade. Believe me, I know.

Blood dripped down Raj's chin like juice from a ripe pomegranate. "Shouldn't you be leaning forward and pinching your nose," I said, "or singing *The Star-Spangled Banner* with your fingers in your ears or something?"

Raj raised his shoulders.

"Wait there," I said. "I'll get you some paper towels from the boys' bathroom. Then I want to talk to you about ghosts and the old lady who used to live in our house."

I ignored Raj's puzzled expression and ducked into the bathroom.

At first I assumed I was the only one in there, but as I was about to leave I noticed a humongous pair of shoes caked with mud poking out from under the toilet stall. Intrigued at the glaring violation of the school dress code, I waited for the footwear to come out, killing time washing my hands.

A few seconds later a guy in a cap and a long, filthy coat over a bright red shirt emerged, and I couldn't stop my jaw from dropping two inches. I must have looked like a goldfish, but the thing was, this guy wasn't just wearing any old clothes. He was wearing a Civil War uniform, and my knees almost buckled under me as I realized I was face to face with my ghost.

Disappearing quicker than candy on Halloween, I rocketed out of the bathroom and into the hallway.

"In there," I stuttered to Raj. "The ghost, he's in there."

Raj was not happy. "And my paper towels would be where?"

"Never mind that. I saw him again. The ghost. A Civil War guy covered head to toe in mud."

"Confederate or Union?" asked Raj.

"I don't know. Is that important?" I snapped.

"I was kidding," said Raj, wiping his bloody nose on his sleeve. "There are no ghosts in our school. How about you and me take a teenie weenie walk and go and see the nursie. Okay?"

"I don't need to see the nurse," I cried. "*I'm* fine. But I'm telling you, there's a Civil War soldier standing right there in the bathroom taking a pee. Go and see for yourself, if you don't believe me."

"A Civil War ghost?" Raj tipped his head to the side again. I wasn't sure if that was because he didn't believe me, or if it helped stop the blood.

"Go," I said, pushing him in the direction of the boys' bathrooms.

Raj vanished down the hall, spraying DNA liberally as he went, returning five minutes later with a handful of towels and a trailing ghost.

"Jake, I'd like you to meet Mr. Watts, our new drama teacher." Raj beamed at me like I was an idiot. "He's in costume. They're in the middle of a dress rehearsal."

Mr. Watts thrust out his hand. "Hi, Jake. Raj, here, says you'd be very interested in taking part in our school play, *A Camp Divided.* We've always got room for eager thespians."

Being a kid who'd rather have his fingernails pulled out one by one than speak in front of an audience, I didn't think so.

"I'll pass, thanks," I said.

"Well, if you change your mind, let me know," said the drama teacher before clumping off down the hallway whistling *Yankee Doodle*, badly.

"Nice one, Raj," I said sarcastically.

"You're welcome." His nose had stopped bleeding. "Do you still believe in this ghost?"

"Yes," I said, digging into my back pocket and extracting the folded up piece of yellowed paper. "Take a look at this."

Raj read the fractured sentences. "It seems to be part of a letter. It looks very old. Where did you get it?"

"The ghost left it," I said.

"The ghost left it?" echoed Raj, his eyes as white and round as a pair of new golf balls.

"Yes. Last night. I think he was in my room during the power cut."

Raj shook his head in disbelief as we started walking back toward the lockers. The bell was about to ring. "I'm certain the weird stuff going on at my place is a ghost haunting our property and I think it has something to do with the shadow of the noose I saw in my bedroom. Maybe he left this note for me as a clue."

"A clue to what?" asked Raj.

"I don't know," I said. "That's the problem."

"You're serious, aren't you?" said Raj.

I nodded as we reached the lockers and I punched in my code on my locker.

Raj leaned heavily against the metal casing. "Dadaji says you should never mess with the dead, and you should beware of the man's shadow and the bee's sting," he said in a serious tone.

"Then we'll just have to be careful." I smiled nervously.

But Raj was not smiling. "I don't want anything to do with this." He handed me back the scrap of paper. "There's the bell. I'll see you at lunch."

As we drifted down the hall to our separate classes, I wondered, was Raj right? Was it taboo to mess with spirits? I mean, what harm could it do? After all, it wasn't like he wanted to murder me or anything.

Right?

Chapter Six

Hanging Around

Later, at lunch, I met up with Raj in the cafeteria. Unfortunately, Tiger Stone and his herd chose to sit with us, too, and it didn't take long to realize we weren't going to be discussing the political correctness of the term French fries. But my mind was elsewhere thinking about ghosts.

"I see you had a conversation with Alan Idle," Tiger said to Raj over the roar of ravenous students. "Like I said, I can help you, but it works both ways. What do *you* say, Jake Salmon. Do you think your friend here made a good choice?"

I blinked away the image of the rebellious ghoul. "Sorry, Tiger, were you talking to me?"

"He's being funny." Tiger punched one of his pals on the shoulder, knocking him sideways off his chair. "Our little friend has a sense of humor. We like that, don't we?"

The farm animals nodded. I laughed, too. I could be pretty funny.

I punched Raj playfully on his shoulder. Raj frowned.

Tiger, leaning over the table stickier than a fly strip, his hand skirting around the puddles of congealed ketchup, swiped my lunch tray to the side. "Don't get smart with me," he said. Adopting a more pleasant tone, he continued, "But

38

you'll be pleased to know, I've changed my mind about the test."

Finally things were looking up for Raj.

"Yeah," said Tiger. "I've thought of another way my little Indian friend can help me."

So I was wrong.

"Next Tuesday afternoon," he drawled, "me and the guys need to get out of school early, so we need someone to create a diversion."

"What sort of a diversion?" said Raj, nervously.

"Like a fire or something," Tiger said.

"You want me to start a fire?" Raj's eyes bulged out of his head.

Tiger got up from the table and came round to our side. He ruffled Raj's raven hair and with a jerk of his head instructed me wordlessly to move over and make room. As I slid sideways, he flung his beefy arm around Raj's shoulders. "Raj Gupta, would we ask you to do something as irresponsible as start a fire?" His barnyard brood laughed like he'd cracked the funniest joke on the planet. "No, no, no. I just thought you could accidentally set off the fire alarm. No biggie. Accidents happen. What do ya think?"

"You want me to set off the fire alarm so you can skip school?" Beads of sweat danced on Raj's forehead.

"You catch on quick," Tiger said. "I like you."

For Raj's sake I wish Tiger didn't.

"I'll think about it," said Raj.

"Good boy." Tiger Stone beamed and rose from the table. His pals beamed too. It was like one big party, only somehow my friend had assumed the role of the piñata about to be smashed to a pulp.

As Tiger departed, Raj turned his face to mine. "What choice did I have?" he wailed. "There's only so much blood a kid can lose. Dadaji says, do not blame God for having created the tiger, but thank him for not having given it wings."

I downed my chocolate milk in one gulp.

"You know what, Raj? Enough already. How about we stop with the proverbs, okay?"

We finished the rest of our lunch in silence.

At the end of a very long day, the three o'clock bell pealed our release from academics, and on the walk home with Danny, invisible Edward, and Raj, I brought up the subject of the ghost again.

"You can't be serious," said Raj. "How can I be thinking about your ghost when I'm in training to be a pyromaniac?"

"What's a pyromaniac?" asked Danny.

"It's someone who starts fires on purpose," said Raj.

"Will the police come and take you away?" asked Danny.

"Yes," said Raj, sighing. "Will you come and visit me?"

"Edward hates prisons," said Danny.

"Don't worry. I'll think of something," I said. I had no idea what though. I wish I wasn't such a coward. But it was in my genes, and I was not referring to my Levis. I picked up a stick and let it trail behind me in the snow as we walked. "I googled ghosts during activity period this morning," I said, stamping in the snow. "Imagine a body without bones, flesh and organs, just a voice, a smell, a spirit and a soul. That's a ghost."

"Neat," said Danny, "What else did it say?"

"That they can pass through solid objects."

"Edward's good at that," said Danny. Raj threw a snowball at him.

"I think the ghost must have passed through the basement door before floating across the backyard. It also said that they can be seen and heard by some people, but not others. That's why Mom couldn't hear anything, but we could," I said. I kicked a cloud of snow into the air, causing a mini snowstorm. "The other thing I read was that sometimes, when there is a ghost present, you feel extremes of temperature—and I've felt a shiver each time I came across the ghost."

"Assuming this is for real," said Raj, finally getting into it. "I thought spirits or ghosts only appear for a reason."

"They do," I said, now an expert. "It could be because they're seeking revenge, or they're guarding over the premises, or they want a truth to be uncovered."

"So what do you think your ghost wants?" asked Raj.

I stopped walking and grabbed Raj by the arm. "That's the problem, Raj. I don't know. But I have a feeling he's not going to leave until we do."

We were at Raj's house. I saw the beady eyes of his grandfather peering out behind the sheers.

"Can you tell I got hit in the face?" Raj asked, turning to me.

I scanned his nose for marks. "Nope, you're fine."

"Thanks. See you," said Raj.

"Wait, I still haven't asked you about the woman we bought the house from. Can you come over to my place later?"

"Sure," Raj called as he disappeared up his front steps to confront Dadaji.

Within the hour Raj and I sat on the front porch tossing snowballs at the oak tree. Danny was having a snowball fight with Edward, who, apparently, had bad aim, which explained why Danny never got hit.

"So, what do you know about the old lady who used to live here?" I asked Raj.

"You mean Mrs. Snell?" said Raj. "I remember she had a face like a scrunched up paper bag and she was really tiny, about as tall as Danny."

"Did you ever speak to her?" I asked.

"Nah. She lived on her own, and I hardly ever saw her outside. I think she was either British, or Australian. I did visit her house last year for trick or treat, though. That was a mistake."

I grabbed a handful of wet snow and formed it into a perfect sphere. "Why, did she hand out toothbrushes instead of candy? I hate that."

"No, it was nothing like that. I was shadowing a horde of preschool Elvis Presleys. They were laughing and skipping and seemed pretty happy with the old lady's handouts, so I thought this was one of the good houses, you know."

"Sure." I nodded in agreement. It was key to hit on the generous givers—the dads who handed out multiple Snickers bars, or the old cronies who would buy mega bags of candy to attract the big numbers. There was an elderly lady in our last neighborhood who would pay you to come to her house, but she was a rare breed.

Raj continued, "So I assumed this was *the* house for the mega candy."

"I'd have done the same," I said, nibbling a lump of snow.

"I rang the bell, had my pillowcase open at the ready, smeared extra ketchup across my face in the hope of a bonus Mars Bar, and waited. Through the glass in the front door, I could see her shuffling down the hall."

I nodded. We'd all been there. The anticipation of Halloween treats was one of life's simple pleasures.

"Eventually, the door swings open and I'm staring at wrinkles and hair the color of a dime. I adopted my widest smile and said, 'Happy Halloween.' But she took one look at me and screamed loud enough to wake the dead."

"But you were dressed as a cereal killer last year, weren't you?" I said. "What's so scary about a load of crushed Cheerio boxes stuck to your sweater?"

"No clue. *She* was more frightening. Then she slammed the door in my face and the next day the 'Sale' sign went up. Am I really that scary?"

"Absolutely," I said, without hesitation. "But no one sells their house because of an ugly kid or because the neighborhood supports lousy Halloween costumes. There had to be another reason Mrs. Snell sold to us at such a low price. Do you know where she moved to? I wonder if she stayed in the area."

"She did," said Raj. "She moved into the retirement center on Payne Lane. Dadaji has a lady friend there, and he drags me along with him sometimes. I saw Mrs. Snell once. I didn't hang around. I didn't want to give her a heart attack." He made an exaggerated shudder.

We lived on Fayette Street, and Payne Lane was just a few blocks away. The street map of our small town, littered with roads named after Civil War heroes, read like a Civil War regiment.

I hurled a handful of snow into the air. Danny yelled at me for hitting Edward. "I suggest we go and pay her a visit," I said. My butt was beginning to freeze to the step.

"You can count me out," said Raj. "I hate that place. It's got a weird smell."

"That's stupid," I said. "You have to come. You can take a bunch of flowers to your grandfather's friend, and I'll see if we can chat to the old lady."

The next day we paid a visit to Mrs. Snell.

Plantation Retirement Center was a one-story building a fifteen-minute walk from our house. From the outside it looked like Danny's old preschool, *Free To Be Me*. It had a large parking lot with more than half the spots allocated to handicapped parking. If Dad had been with us, he'd have moaned about that. He always did. A sign outside invited us all to Bingo, on Saturdays at three. Adjacent to the sign stood two rusty cannons. We brought Danny along too—little kids are always a plus around old people. Danny didn't invite Edward. He said Edward had an ear infection.

Raj was the first through the glass door. The foyer was warm and bright and smelled of fresh paint. A woman sitting behind a reception desk, wearing a green sweater with a picture of a cat on it, popped up from behind a large potted plant. She smiled when she recognized Raj.

"Good morning, Raj, how nice to see you. Is your grandfather not with you today?" Her earrings, in the shape of Siamese cats, dangled like Christmas tree ornaments as she spoke.

"No, but he asked me to bring these flowers to his friend," said Raj in his politest voice. He shuffled his feet uncomfortably. It had taken considerable effort to persuade Raj to lie.

"What a good child you are," said the cat fan. "You know where to go, right?"

The red-jeweled eyes on her cat earrings started flashing on and off. The woman appeared to be connected to the electricity.

Raj, ignoring the light display, held his bunch of pink, lacy flowers in front of him and charged down the hallway. We followed.

About halfway down, Danny touched a painting on the wall of a field of poppies. It crashed to the floor.

"What are you doing?" I groaned. "We were trying not to draw attention to ourselves."

"It wasn't hanging straight," said Danny.

"Quite right," said a croaky voice from the room next to where the picture had fallen as an old woman appeared. She came up to my armpit and had a face like chewed Bazooka bubblegum. "That painting has been driving me crackers ever since I moved in here." She pointed her hooked finger at Raj. "I've seen you here before with your grandfather visiting Mrs. Lamb. She's a terrible cheat at cards, you know." The old lady pulled at Raj's sleeve. "And a beggar for eating all the biscuits." She sounded like the Queen of England.

Raj smiled politely as her watery eyes landed on me and Danny. "And who might these young gentlemen be? I don't think I've seen you bairns here before."

"We're with him," I said, nodding to Raj, who was winking his right eye as if he had some rare twitching disease.

"And what do they call you, lads?" she said.

"I'm Jake Salmon, and this is my brother Danny."

The old lady held out her hand. I shook it gently, frightened it might snap off. Her skin felt as fragile as tissue paper—the shiny kind that you find in birthday gift bags.

"Ah, the Salmon boys. You bought my house. How do you do," she said. "I'm Mrs. Snell. I wondered how long it would take you to find me. Why don't you come along and have a chat with me while your friend here takes those lovely carnations to Mrs. Lamb."

"That's what I was trying to tell you," whispered Raj in my ear before disappearing down the hallway. "That's Mrs. Snell."

"Come on, lads, don't hang about," she said, motioning us to follow her inside her lair. "I've been expecting you for some time."

Chapter Seven

Mrs. Snell

Mrs. Snell's living room didn't have much furniture. There was a sofa, an armchair, a tiny TV, and a grandfather clock in the corner. She didn't have a GameCube or a PlayStation. But I did notice a computer on a small wooden table by the window. The room smelled of cold, brown gravy. I thought I was going to puke at first, but then I sort of got used to the odor.

"Why don't you lads sit on the settee, and I'll get you both a cup of squash and some biscuits." She tottered off into an adjoining room, reappearing a few minutes later with a tray with two glasses of orange juice, a plate of tiny cookies, and a cup of tea in a fancy cup and saucer.

She handed us our snack and placed the china cup on the side table by the large knobby armchair.

"I expect you're here about the ghost?" She lowered herself at glacial speed into the armchair. We nodded vigorously.

"What a tale that is. Let me tell you. At first I thought it was the local kids up to no good," she said. "Every night, just after midnight, I'd awake to slamming and clanking coming from down in the cellar."

"What's a cellar?" asked Danny, standing up and walking over to the windowsill where Mrs. Snell displayed a collection of shiny buttons and coins.

"A basement to you," she said.

"Are you from New Jersey?" Danny asked, firing the questions at her like bullets from a gun.

"My giddy Aunt, whatever gave you such a notion? No, I'm from England."

Danny picked up a gold button. "Where did you get this?" he asked. "It's from a Virginian Civil War uniform."

"How does a little tot like you know something like that?" said Mrs. Snell. "I found that one in the front yard by the old oak tree. I collect them, you see. Do you think it might be valuable?"

"Maybe." Danny ran his fingers over the smooth surface.

"Buttons tell you many things about an era," she added, smiling. I had a feeling she was about to tell us a story about the good old days. You have to watch it with ancient people or you can lose hours of time.

"So what happened when you heard the noises in the basement?" I prompted.

"Well, you see my cat, Snowy, over there—"

A gigantic white cotton ball observed us with bored, green eyes.

"—she's thirteen, an old lady just like me," Mrs. Snell chortled. "And set in her ways, too, she is. Well, she started acting right peculiar. She wouldn't go into certain parts of certain rooms. She refused point blank to go into the cellar with me—which she'd never done before. Then her hair started sticking up—just like yours does, pet."

Danny thought his spiky hair was cool. I thought he looked like he'd had a hundred bolts of electricity shot through his skull.

"And that was when it occurred to me that my house might be haunted. I mentioned it to Hank Creek—"

"Who's Hank Creek?" I asked.

"The postman, but he's a right gossip, he is. And the next thing, local kids are skirting my property calling me the English witch. But I didn't take any notice. I had my Snowy. Then I got to thinking, maybe the ghost was trying to communicate with me. You have to understand, I'd lived in that house for over thirty years with no sign of a ghost. The first time he appeared was the day I decided to have the old oak tree in the front yard removed." She scratched her chin as she worked out the dates. "Yes, it was last autumn. I'd never heard a peep from the old ghost before that, then I try and have the oak tree removed and, Bob's your uncle, I disturb a sleeping ghoul."

"Why did you want to cut the tree down?" I asked.

"Because Snowy was a devil for climbing that tree and getting stuck. She's afraid of heights, you see."

"But the tree's still there," Danny said, helping himself to his tenth cookie.

"I know. Three times the tree removal people tried to come. The first time their truck got a flat tire and they never made it. The second time the owner was rushed into hospital with appendicitis, and the third time, when they did make it to my house, this very nice chap climbed the tree to chop off the top branches, lost his balance, and fell right out. He landed with one heck of a thud. He was quite delirious when they took him off in the ambulance, muttering something about being pushed from the branch. I never heard from them again. It was that evening I started hearing the noises in the basement. Soon after, I knew we had ourselves a ghost." She paused and dipped her voice so we had to lean in closer to hear her. "Let me warn you right now. That ghost is no good. He's pure evil."

"Why, what happened?" I asked.

She took a sip of her tea. The china cup rattled so much in its saucer I thought for a second we were experiencing an earthquake. I saw a shudder go through Mrs. Snell.

"Now, don't get me wrong. I'd have been quite happy to stay there if he'd kept to himself," she said in a thoughtful voice. "But he was a right bugger. He would creep up on me. Open and close the cupboard doors right when I was in the middle of my TV soaps. Then my cat went missing for a couple of days. I hunted high and low. Couldn't find her anywhere. Do you know where she was?"

We shook our heads. We had no idea.

"In the dryer," said Mrs. Snell, her loose skin flapping in outrage as she flung her arms up in the air. I looked over at Danny, willing him not to cry. "Then the next day the bloody ghost pushes me down the stairs. I thought I'd tripped the first time, but the third time he got cocky and showed himself. The little scoundrel stood there laughing as I tumbled like Jack and Jill. I was lucky not to break my neck. And a mischievous face he had too. He needed a good shower and a shave. I could see from his clothing he was a soldier."

"Did you find out what he wanted?" I asked.

"I came close," she said. "I knew it had something to do with the tree. I'd been seeing this strange shadow like a noose hanging from its limbs—"

"I see that too!" I said, unable to contain the excitement in my voice. "All the time. What did you think it meant?"

Mrs. Snell put down her cup and saucer gently on the side table and moistened her faded lips with her catlike, pink tongue. "Well, I searched under 'Civil War Skirmishes' in this area on Google dot com—"

"The Internet?" I was unable to hide my astonishment. Old people don't know about the Internet.

"You think because I haven't got me own teeth I can't use a computer?" said Mrs. Snell in a sharp voice. "I'll have you know, pet, I was a code-breaker in England during the war. Have you heard of Bletchley Park?"

I shook my head.

"What do they teach you at school? Bletchley Park is in England and it's where the German top secret codes were broken during World War Two." She tutted and patted the back of her hair.

"We *are* in America," I pointed out.

"Humpf," she grunted. "Well, I think the World Wide Web is bloody brilliant. Did you know you can send an email to the other side of the world and they receive it straight away? I sent one to my sister in England, and she got it before I'd sent it. Amazing." Mrs. Snell's eyes lit up as if she'd uncovered a million dollars.

"So did you find anything out about the ghost?" I pressed.

Mrs. Snell continued, "Of course I knew that Manassas, only a few miles away, was of major importance in the Civil War, but I also discovered that there had been an important battle right in our front yard."

"Wow, I wonder how many soldiers got killed?" said Danny.

"And I saw him again," Mrs. Snell added before taking another sip of her tea, which seemed to take forever. Eventually the cup was reunited with the saucer, and Mrs. Snell laid her hands in her lap and took a deep breath.

"You saw the ghost?" said Danny.

"Not in the flesh. I saw an old photograph on the computer screen of a whole battalion of Civil War soldiers, and there he was, stood right in the middle of the group, his cheeky, whiskery face grinning back at me. A picture of my ghost."

Danny choked down his orange juice. "What color was his jacket, blue or grey?"

"I don't know. The photo was black and white. Ask me about the Battle of Britain, and I can tell you anything you want to know, but get me onto American history and you get more sense from your family parrot. But I did find out our ghost's name. Thomas Garnet."

Garnet? That was a coincidence. Mom's mom was Grandma Garnet.

"Did you find anything else out? Did he get killed in battle?" I asked.

"That's all I know." Mrs. Snell shook her head with a sigh. "Although, let me see. I did find an old poem in my basement. It's over there, in that pile of papers on the windowsill next to the buttons. If I remember correctly, it's dated August 29th 1862."

I stood up and went over to the window and retrieved the few lines of verse.

"So what do you make of it?" Mrs. Snell asked. "Why don't you read it out loud so your brother can hear it?"

I did as I was told.

"The fruit droops from the outstretched limb,
Oscillating, withered, inert,
A bitter taste, the after taste,
Who'd have known in this misdisert
        Robert Black. August 29th 1862"

"I hate poetry," whined Danny in between mouthfuls of more cookies.

"I know what you mean," said Mrs. Snell. "Do you like poems, Jake?"

Ah, hum. I cleared my throat. Lights, camera, action, if you please. I smiled confidently at Mrs. Snell and held out the poem in front of me. "As it happens, I do," I said. "Oscillating means to sway."

"Is that a fact?" said Mrs. Snell, clapping her hands together. "And do you know what the other words mean?"

"Inert means not moving, I guess like dead," I said. "I'm not sure about misdesert. That could be a very old word."

"So it's about a squishy fruit hanging in a tree in a desert?" said Danny. "Well, duh, I could have written that."

Clutching the poem I paced up and down in front of the window. "The thing with poetry," I said, "is that the sentences are often metaphors. That means it says one thing but is referring to something quite different. And look, the date is the same date as the date on our scrap of paper."

"You mean the fruit might actually be a horse or a camel or something?" said Danny.

"Well, yes, I guess, but that doesn't make any sense either. Do you think we could borrow this, Mrs. Snell? I'd like to take it home and scan it into my computer."

"Of course, pet. Just take good care of it. It might be valuable. If you look in the drawer over there, you'll find a large envelope. Pop it in one to protect it, would you?"

"But what made you decide to sell the house?" I asked.

Mrs. Snell drained her tea. "It was after an incident at Halloween last year."

I groaned inwardly. So Raj was to blame after all. "You mean when you saw Raj dressed up as a cereal killer? He didn't mean to scare you," I said.

The old lady let out a hearty chuckle. "Your nice Raj didn't bother me. No, no, no. That night, I went to give a bag of candy to Raj when behind him I saw that raggedy old soldier, Thomas Garnet, swinging from the branch of the old oak tree, a rope around his neck. Only he wasn't dead. He twisted his grisly face towards me, sideways you understand, and winked at me, all bold like. Well, that was enough. My heart's not that strong, and I decided right then and there to sell up and move. But I take it from your visit here today that the old goose is still making a pest of himself."

"Yes, he is," I said.

The large grandfather clock struck three and Mrs. Snell got up and took our cups. "Well, lads, as much as I like the company, I'm going to have to ask you to leave. I'm late for my bingo."

I nodded to Danny to quit eating and picked up our coats from the back of the sofa.

As I reached for the door handle, Mrs. Snell placed her frail hand on my arm and gripped it like she was hanging on for her life. "A word of warning, boys. My advice is to leave well enough alone. He's a bad sort. Nothing good will come of it. You mind my words. And whatever you do, do not chop down that old oak tree."

Chapter Eight

Uprooting

We left Mrs. Snell to her bingo and joined Raj, who'd been waiting for us out in the foyer. We told him we had discovered our ghost had a name, Thomas Garnet.

"According to Mrs. Snell," I said, as we tramped back home, "our house was built on the actual site of a Civil War battle."

"This has been the best day ever." Danny skipped along beside us, his little head bobbing up and down with delight. "I can't wait to tell Edward. I hope he's feeling better. He may need antibiotics."

Danny stopped abruptly, bent down, then dragged his hand along the sidewalk scooping up a ball of snow and chucking it over a fence at a plastic swan.

I suddenly had a thought. "If Thomas Garnet was one of the soldiers killed in battle, why is he the only one haunting the property? Why would one soldier come back to haunt and not another?"

I remembered that Mrs. Snell had said she'd seen Thomas Garnet hanging in a noose from the oak tree in her front yard. "Maybe Thomas Garnet didn't die in battle," I said. "Maybe he was hanged?"

"But why?" said Raj. "What could he have done? Surely they needed all the manpower they could get during a skirmish."

"I don't know," I said. "But I'm starting to think that if we chop down our tree he'll haunt us forever." We rounded the corner close to home. "Maybe even try and kill one of us, like he did to Mrs. Snell."

Our front yard came into view, and I could see Dad sitting in the driver's seat of his red Chevy truck. But something was wrong. It was parked at an odd angle facing out into the middle of the road with its back wheels on the edge of the yard, its engine revving. A taught rope connected the bumper and the oak tree.

What on earth? I couldn't believe it. Dad was having another go at the tree.

"No," I yelled, running down the street. "Stop, Dad! You can't do that."

I reached the truck and hammered on the window pane. But the truck screamed as the tires spun around and around in the snow, foraging into the earth, cutting deep tracks into the sod. I flung open the passenger door and jumped up beside Dad. The engine sounded like it would explode at any second, straining like a horse desperate to escape the reins of a brutal owner. Then a crack louder than the biggest firework on the Fourth of July burst our ear drums, and the truck catapulted forward. Everything happened in slow motion. Suddenly I couldn't breathe—you know like when you fall on your back and the wind is knocked out of your lungs—as the truck came to an abrupt halt. Dad scrambled out and raced around to my side. He forced my door open, slid his arm gently under my body, and with the ease of a giant picking up a peanut he lifted me clear of the truck. His face looked like it had been ravaged by a wild animal. Blood dripped down his cheeks onto my coat.

"I'm so sorry, Jake," Dad said, parking me gently on the front step. "Are you okay?"

"I'm fine. I couldn't breathe there for a while, but I think I'm okay." I looked up into his face. "You're bleeding onto my coat, Dad."

He put his hand up to feel his forehead. "I must have hit the windshield. That was pretty stupid, wasn't it?" He looked up. Mom was approaching. "Now I'm in for it. Cover for me, will you. Say it was the ghost."

For a second I thought Dad was serious, then I realized he was just trying to make me feel better.

Mom insisted I go inside and lie down for a while as my chest hurt. She followed me inside as I traipsed upstairs to my bedroom.

"How are you feeling?" she asked as she sat down on my bed smoothing my hair to one side like she was preparing me for picture day.

"I'm fine," I said. "What happened exactly?"

"The back bumper of the truck tore off, causing the vehicle to shoot forward," she said. "Your dad is going to go to the hospital. He may need stitches."

My bedroom door flew open as Danny came rushing into the room holding a magazine and a piece of cardboard with the words "Company Q" written on it in bold black letters. He sidled up to the bed.

"I thought you might like something to read," he said.

"Thanks, Danny," I said. It was the latest copy of *The Civil War Times*. "What's the placard for?"

"I'm going to hang this on your door. Company Q was the name for the sick list for the Confederate army."

"Sweet," I said.

Mom walked over to the window and gazed out. It had started to snow again, erasing all the sharp edges. The tracks of the afternoon's activity would soon vanish under a fresh, white sheet like it had never happened.

"Why was Dad trying to pull down the tree?" I asked.

"Oh, you know your dad. If he gets a bee in his bonnet about something there's no stopping him." Mom had her back to me at the window.

"Is he still going to chop it?" I said.

She came away from the window, collapsed at the foot of my bed, and took Danny's hand, pulling him onto her knee. "No. I think he's finally admitted defeat. He always hated flowering cherry trees anyway."

I suddenly felt very tired. I glanced at Mom cuddling Danny and found myself wanting to be Danny's age so that she'd pull me into the folds of her soft pink sweater. I wanted to tell her about Raj and the bullying at school, and how I never got a full night's sleep thanks to a crazy ghost.

"You okay, Jake? If you need to talk—" Mom had on her worried face.

"Nah, it's just allergies," I said, wiping my eyes with the back of my hand.

"I'll go and make us some nice chicken soup," said Mom, sliding Danny off her knee. Mom left us alone.

Danny had a weird expression on his face.

"What's up, Danny? I'm gonna be okay. I'm only bruised, and Dad will be back from the hospital soon."

He was fiddling with something in his hand.

"What's that?" I asked him.

Danny held his hand out flat. In the middle of his small palm rested a gold button.

"That's Mrs. Snell's Civil War button. Did you steal it?"

Danny's bottom lip started to tremble. "I didn't mean to. I forgot I had it in my hand."

"Don't worry. We'll go back to the retirement home tomorrow and give it back. You won't get in trouble. How's Edward's ear infection?" I asked, changing the subject.

Danny stared at me. At first I thought he hadn't heard me. Then he picked up his felt infantry hat lying on his bed and spoke to the rug.

"Edward's not here anymore," he said. "He's dead."

"What do you mean, dead?"

"He got squished under Dad's truck," he said.

Okay.

Chapter Nine

Dropping Like Flies

The next morning Danny and I returned to Plantation Retirement Center. The lady in reception had switched her cat theme for zoo animals. Zebras swayed from her earlobes matching her black and white striped sweater.

"Hello," she said in a kind voice, closing a magazine she was looking at. "You back again?"

"We need to see Mrs. Snell. We have something for her," I said fingering the button in my pocket.

"Ah." The receptionist stood up and came around to the front of her desk, then knelt down to Danny's height. "I'm afraid Mrs. Snell is no longer with us, hon'."

"What do you mean?" I asked. "Has she moved? She didn't tell us she was going anywhere." I took a step back and peered up the hallway half expecting to see her crooked shape.

"No, I mean Mrs. Snell has passed," she said in a quiet voice.

"Passed what?" said Danny.

The lady let out a huge sigh. "Passed away. Mrs. Snell died yesterday evening, in her sleep. She was very, very old," she added quickly.

Mrs. Snell dead. But that couldn't be. She was fine yesterday.

"Was she shot?" asked Danny.

"Oh bless your heart, no," said the receptionist, going back behind her desk and shuffling some papers into a neat pile.

I placed both my hands on the front of her desk and looked directly at her. "Then how did she die?"

"I believe she had a heart attack," she said, picking up and looking through a file on her desk. "But I'm sure it was very peaceful. I had already gone home for the day. I found out this morning when I came in. Were you related to her? I didn't think she had any grandchildren."

I took a hold of Danny's sleeve. "No, we were just her friends. New friends." I took the button out of my pocket and handed it to the lady. "But this belonged to her. We were returning it. It might be valuable. We have a poem of hers too, at home. We'll return it too."

"Thank you," said the receptionist, taking the button and depositing it in a white envelope. "I'll make sure her son gets it when he returns for her things."

Danny suddenly slapped his hand to his mouth. "Oh no, what about her cat, Snowy? Did she die, too?"

The receptionist tilted her head to the side and smiled. "No, dear, Snowy is fine. Mrs. Snell's son took the cat back with him last night."

I took Danny by the hand. "We'd better be going," I said, swallowing the lump in my throat.

Outside Danny's face turned the color of ash. "Do you think she was murdered?"

"Well, if you count being scared to death by a ghost, then yes, I do. I think Thomas Garnet came here last night."

"But why?" said Danny. "I don't understand."

"Because he was furious with her about what she told us." I plucked a leaf from a nearby hedge and tore it into thin shreds. "She was our only human witness. I wonder who'll be next."

That night, at around three in the morning, Thomas Garnet returned. My chest hurt so much I couldn't get comfortable and was having a hard time getting to sleep. It felt like I'd swallowed a pair of scissors. Just as I drifted off, the sound of clapping outside my window caused me to start. I crept painfully out of bed and peered out. A full moon illuminated the fresh snow and I saw a shadowy form in the branches of the white oak. I eased myself into a sweatshirt and stole downstairs. Slipping on my shoes without socks and grabbing a flashlight from the shelf above the key rack, I silently unlocked the front door and let myself out.

As I shone the flashlight up into the tree the clap, clap, clap cracked through the stillness like jumping jacks. My hands trembled but not from the cold. Should I have woken my brother? What if I perished without trace? Would Mom give my CD player to Danny? I should have left a note. I'd much rather Raj got it.

A cloud passed over the full moon like an ominous warning. I looked up into the dark limbs and saw that the shadowy figure was no longer in the body of the tree but dangling on the end of a rope tied to a branch, swaying, in time to the steady beat of its own applause. In the beam of light I saw his eyes were closed but he wasn't dead. He clapped his hands together, slowly, rhythmically. I edged nearer and circled his body. This was the closest I'd ever been to Thomas Garnet. A few inches from his gaunt face I held out my hand to touch him. Then an eye opened and the hanging body winked at me and grinned, his meager rows of teeth resembling a piano keyboard.

I let out a scream and sat up, then screamed again from the pain.

I was in bed. It had been a dream. I was covered in sweat.

"Be quiet," groaned the tired voice of my brother nearby.

"Danny, Danny. Wake up," I whispered.

"No."

"Danny, I just had the worst dream. Do you want to hear about it?" I asked.

"No."

"I dreamed I saw Thomas Garnet hanging in the tree outside. He was wearing a soldier's uniform."

"Which side?" asked the sleepy voice.

"His jacket was grey. That's Confederate, isn't it? Danny, it was a dream but I know it meant something."

I tried to go back to sleep but I had an eerie sensation that Danny and I were not alone in the room. In the half light I felt someone close to me. A shadow knelt by my bed. I stiffened in fear and tried to call out, but no words came.

"Help me, help me," the ghost whispered, but as quickly as it had appeared it vanished.

Mustering all my strength I rolled out of bed and stumbled to the window. Outside it looked exactly as it had in my dream, except without the body in the tree and no clapping. But then I noticed something in the snow by the base of the tree like a piece of colored rag.

I grabbed a notepad from my desk and scribbled, "In the event of my disappearance give my new CD player to Raj Gupta," and limped downstairs and outside.

Still expecting to witness the dead body suspended from the branch, it was a relief to see the tree was nothing more than a tree. But when I searched the ground I discovered a rectangular cut of material stiff from lying in the snow. I held it up and saw it was an American flag, but it had only seven stars and three wide stripes, two red, and one white. Next to the flag, traced in the snow, was a shape of a heart. What did it mean?

I stumbled back inside, shivering, and shook Danny awake.

"Go away," he said without opening his eyes.

"I have something you'd be interested in," I teased.

Danny peeked through one eye, his head not leaving his pillow. As soon as he saw the flag dangling in front of him he bolted upright. "That's a Confederate Stars and Bars flag. Where did you get it?"

"It was under the tree outside. How do you know it's a Confederate flag?"

Danny touched the material like he was fingering pure gold. "Because the Union flag had more stars and more stripes. It had thirty-five stars for the thirty-five states in the Union.

"It was an honor for a soldier to carry the flag," Danny murmured in a sleepy voice. "But that was a very dangerous position, because holding the flag made you an easy target."

How did he memorize all this stuff?

"Maybe we should visit the Battlefield Museum," I said, "and see what we can find out about Thomas Garnet. We have a day off school next Friday for the end of the marking period. We could go into work with Mom."

"Good idea," Danny yawned. Then he took the flag, and folding it carefully laid it under his pillow next to his sword. "I'll take care of this." In seconds he was back dreaming.

I had to put all thoughts of the ghost aside the next day, when at school, we were welcomed with the news from the principal, Monty Moon, that someone was breaking into lockers and stealing stuff.

"We have a thief among us," Dr. Moon announced at morning assembly.

Hello? Welcome to the real world of middle school.

"But I am prepared to give whoever is responsible a chance to own up, anonymously," he said. "This lunchtime, I shall take a stroll outside. I will leave my office unlocked and if the person who has been pilfering could return the items and place them on my desk, no more will be said."

That lunchtime, Principal Moon's jar of M & Ms was stolen from his office.

After the sixth period Raj and I hurried to our lockers. We had been successfully avoiding Tiger and Alan, but just as we were retreating from the lockers, Tiger Stone sauntered up.

"One word," he said.

"Antidisestablishmentarianism?" I suggested, feeling brave.

"Uh, no," said Tiger in a confused voice. "Fire alarm."

"That's two words," said Raj.

Now we were pushing it.

Clouds of steam spurted out of Tiger's ears. "When are you going to set it off?" He poked Raj in the shoulder.

"He's working on it, okay?" I said in a confident voice, disguising the fact that my insides were running all over the place. "Come on, Raj. We're late."

Down the hallway, leaving Tiger behind us, Raj turned to me. "Thanks, Jake," he said simply.

I'd stood up to Tiger. I'd actually had the last word. Who'd have thought it?

"You're welcome," I said. "You're not really going to set off the alarm, are you?"

"No. Of course not."

"We could talk to a teacher. Mr. Finch is really nice. I'm sure he'd help," I suggested.

"No way. I'm not telling a teacher," said Raj as we reached the classroom. "Have you had any more ghost attacks?"

I told Raj about the flag and the markings in the snow. "I'm going to ask my mom to take us with her to work. To the

Battlefield Park. I want to dig around in the archives. See what we can find out about Thomas Garnet and Robert Black, the author of the poem. Are you in?"

"Fate and self-help share equally in shaping our destiny," said Raj.

"Words of wisdom from Dadaji?" I asked. "What's it mean?"

"Not a clue, but I guess I'll come to Manassas. I owe you."

Close to the end of the school day, I could barely breathe, my chest hurt so much, so I decided to go to the school nurse to get permission to go home early. It was the middle of a period and the school hallways were as silent as a graveyard. But by my locker, getting my gear for home, I heard footsteps a few rows away.

About halfway down, with his back to me, was Tiger Stone. But he didn't notice me. He was stashing an armful of electronic equipment and a jar of M & Ms into a locker. But the strange thing was he was nowhere near *his* locker. He was hiding the stuff in Alan Idle's locker.

What could this mean? Were Alan Idle and Tiger Stone in on something together? What chance did Raj have if those two teamed up? This was not good. Not good at all.

Chapter Ten

Bingo!

"What a lovely day," Mom said the next morning as she was clearing away the breakfast dishes. "Look outside. The sun has already melted most of the snow." She started to hum.

Would the sun magically melt away a hostile ghost or the school bullies? I didn't think so.

"We need to leave in five minutes. I have to drop something off in Manassas before we head over to the Battlefield Park," said Mom. "Is Raj expecting us to pick him up?"

I walked out into the hallway and grabbed my coat from the hat rack. "No, he said he'd be here. I'll go outside and see if he's coming."

"Did you brush your teeth?" shouted Mom behind me. We both knew the answer to that question.

Outside, in the morning sunshine, the oak tree looked about as scary as a Mary's little lamb. I spotted Raj ambling along the sidewalk heading toward our house.

"Hey, dude," I hollered. "Who we gonna call?"

"Huh?" Raj had a vacant expression.

"Ghost busters," I sang.

"Yeah, right." Raj's heart just wasn't in this, I could tell.

Within a few minutes, Danny, Raj, and I piled into Mom's old red Buick and we set off to the Battlefield Park.

"I'm impressed, Jake," said Mom, as we drove through Old Town Manassas, past the abandoned red-brick candy factory and the old Opera House. "I'm pleased you're finally taking an interest in the history of this country and have stopped with that silly ghost nonsense."

I gave Raj the "look" to keep quiet. I thought it best not to mention our quest. The Battlefield Park visitor's center was less than ten minutes out of town. In one blink the giant-sized M of McDonald's gave way to dormant cannons. From a distance the wooden fences surrounding the Park looked like stitching on a patchwork quilt.

Mom rocked into the parking lot, and we tumbled out the car.

"Why don't you run around outside for a little," Mom suggested, "while I sort out my desk and check my emails. Then I'll take you up to the room where we keep the archives."

"Race you to Henry House," said Danny.

"Sure. Ready, set, go," I said, and watched Danny dart away. "He won't notice we're not running until he gets to the tree. He never does."

A few minutes later we joined Danny. He was splayed out on the ground making a snow angel in one of the few remaining patches of snow. "I won," he declared.

"Yes, you did, Danny. Good job," I said.

"Why is this called Henry Hill?" asked Raj.

"Because there was a huge battle here called the Battle of First Manassas, and this house belonged to the Henry family. The second battle took place in August the next year,"

Danny continued. "It only lasted three days, but almost three thousand men died."

I remembered the scrap of paper. "What year was that, Danny?"

"1862. August 1862," he said.

"That's the date on the torn note and also the poem," I said.

"Did you know," Danny continued, "that to be a soldier in the army you had to have at least four teeth, two on the top and two on the bottom?" He was a bottomless pit of information.

"You're making that up," I said.

"Honest. They had to be able to tear off the paper around the bullets." Danny loved all this.

"What else do you know?" asked Raj. He needed a brother of his own, then he would know the rules. You don't encourage them to talk.

"The shoes they wore were all the same size and the same shape. There was no right or left foot. That way if one got ruined they could just replace it from a dead soldier's foot."

"What happened to the family that lived in this house?" asked Raj with genuine interest.

"The old lady who lived here was sick and refused to leave and got shot. She was the only one who wasn't a soldier to die in the fighting."

I sniffed as my nose ran from the cold and I stamped my feet in an effort to get warm. There were not many trees around and even though the sun was shining, the wind was brutal.

"Let's head back to the visitor's center," I said, "and see if Mom will let us examine the archives."

The archive room was a small, dusty attic with a slanted roof at the top of the visitor's center. Vast vertical files cramped the floor space and filled the walls.

Danny read aloud the sign above the door, "Danger, Maximum Clearance, 5'5"."

"Wow, there are so many books in here. How lucky are we that you're the curator," Raj said to my mom.

"It is open to the public, too," she said, crouching slightly to get through the doorway, "but only by special arrangement. What exactly are you looking for, boys?"

Danny had slipped into the side room and was wrapped around a book that was bigger than his head.

"We have a project on the Battle of Second Manassas, don't we, Raj?" I nudged Raj in the elbows. "And our teacher said there were many diaries and letters belonging to some of the soldiers. Where would we find stuff like that?"

"Okay, boys. A great deal of data is available from many sources. Thousands of pages of correspondence were recorded in the official records of both armies, orders of inquiry and arrests. You could certainly start there." Mom directed us to a whole wall of dusty, brown-backed books. "Here are biographies, *The Committee on the Conduct of the War accounts*, *Confederate Veteran* magazines—"

"What's behind the red door over there?" I pointed to a door on the far side.

"That room houses original documents and journals made by the soldiers, including memoirs and letters. They are very valuable. We keep that room locked. You may go anywhere else, but not there," said Mom.

I noticed the key was still in the lock. That was like being told to help yourself to any of the candy in the store except the jar with the biggest, gooiest, chocolate-covered taffies in the corner with the big sign above saying "Eat Me."

Mom left the room, closing the door behind her. I raised my eyebrows and glanced at Raj.

"No," he said. "Your Mom said we can't."

"Yes, but she didn't mean we couldn't, just that we have to be careful," I said.

"No, she said we couldn't," yelled Danny from the other room.

"I'll tell you what." It was exhausting working with these two. "You can read through the seven hundred books on the shelves over there, and I'll, very carefully, take a peek at the original documents. Just a peek. I'll hardly touch them," I promised.

With a momentary look behind my shoulder just to make sure Mom wasn't lurking under the desk—she has been known to do that, anyone would think she didn't trust me—I opened the red door. The room was even smaller and smelled like old people. It had just one large filing cabinet. I slid the drawer open and took out a binder marked *Civil War: The Battle of Second Manassas: Soldiers' Journals.*

After an hour of painstakingly reading through accounts of the weather flipping from unbearable heat to days of rain, detailing what the soldiers ate for breakfast, and how they couldn't wait to get out and fight, I finally found something.

"Look at this," I called over to Raj. "It's a diary written in August 1862 by a soldier called Robert Black. Remember, that poem the old woman found was written by a Robert Black. In the journal Robert Black refers to his good friend, Tom Garnet." I slammed my hands dramatically on the table. "I think I've found the answer to the mystery of Thomas Garnet."

Chapter Eleven
Primary Sources

Danny took his nose out of his book and raised his head.

"I found a photocopy of an article that mentions Thomas Garnet too," said Raj, waving a sheet of paper in the air.

"You go first," I said.

"The article is an interview with the Confederate general's chief scout, Robert Douglas."

"You mean like a boy scout?" I asked.

"No." Raj shook his head. "Remember last week in social studies, Ms. Browne told us all about the secret spying organization called the Jessie Scouts. Well, that appears to be what Thomas Garnet was. This report describes his capture and interrogation during the Battle of Second Manassas."

"He was a spy?" asked Danny.

"So it says. He was arrested for impersonating an officer. Then they found part of a note detailing plans of the Confederates' most secret maneuvers in Thomas Garnet's knapsack. And once they revealed the scout for who he was, a Union soldier, he was hanged. But Garnet claimed to his last breath he was impersonating an officer simply to impress one of the nurses and had no explanation for the note in his knapsack."

"And this diary appears to agree with that." I held up the frail pages.

Very carefully I knelt down on the ground and laid out three sheets of faded parchment paper on the worn rug. "These are the actual pages of a journal written by the soldier Robert Black from the Seventeenth Virginia Infantry Regiment under General James Longstreet in the Battle of Second Manassas."

Raj and Danny joined me on the ground as I read aloud.

August 25, 1862. I was so stiff this morning it took me a while to stand. I awoke to the sound of the bugle from across the fields. We are positioned by a huge river which provides some relief from the heat. Today we received orders to cook one days rations and be ready to cross the river and march to a town called Salem tomorrow. My friend, Tom Garnet, should be out on look-out, but I'll be willing to wager he's over with his nurse, Emma Dooley. He talks of her all the time, the young fool. Her face is unfamiliar. I saw Tom change into an officer's uniform earlier in the day and head off to the nurses' tent. I should report him for it but the rogue just wants to impress Emma Dooley.

August 26, 1862. I slept out in the open last night. The air was warm and sticky. There is talk of a column of Union cavalry not far off. Brigadier Kemper ordered me to take the guard and march in the rear to catch the stragglers. I have forty men under my charge and I had to drag young Tom Garnet along because the rascal was too drunk to walk. My woolen stockings are thread bare. My blisters bleed. I do not know if I can continue marching. I wrote a letter home today, and Tom Garnet asked me to write a letter to his brother and one to his mother. When I asked why he wouldn't write his own letters, he wouldn't say.

August 27, 1862. The bluebellies are close at hand. We can smell them everywhere. I've been wearing these same clothes now for eight days. I had to drag Tom Garnet out of a brawl last night. He had a nasty gash above his right eye. He was lucky the wound wasn't an inch lower. He'll have a nasty scar but he could have lost his sight. I should have had him arrested for drinking and fighting. He was on guard duty.

"He doesn't sound like a very good soldier," said Danny.

"Well, how would you feel if you had to sleep rough for weeks on end without a change of clothes and no shower?" I said, stretching out my legs.

"I wouldn't care," said Danny. "I hate showers."

"You'd care," I said in an authoritative voice.

"Does he write any more about Thomas Garnet? You haven't got to the first day of the battle yet? Didn't Danny say it started August twenty-eighth?" Raj peered over my shoulder at the papers on the floor.

I traced my forefinger along the words on the page to find my place and continued reading. "This is still the same day."

My blisters hurt so much. Tom Garnet broke rank and ransacked the villages returning with milk, butter and eggs. I should have refused it, or at least asked how he came by it but hunger prevented me. I heard Tom fire a lone shot and I

saw an old village woman chase him across the fields. I heard
her call out, ya'll come back here, what'll I feed my children.
But he out ran her and soon I smelled the fresh steak burning. Brigadier Kemper happened by and said Garnet's be-
havior was that of a Yankee, and he should be ashamed. When
he asked Tom where he'd got the beef, Tom said it was the
spoils of war and grinned as only the young fool can, and
Kemper bellowed, 'It is not in our nature to ransack the homes
of fellow southerners.' But we all lower our standards. I
thought of my own boy back home hungry. I thought of the
old woman with nothing to feed her children and I refused to
eat the meat ignoring my stomach's raging protest.

August 27, 1862. The sun is burning. Today the heat is
unbearable. By nightfall we reached our destination, a small
sleepy town close to the mountains. The skin on my feet is
worn away. We are all so very tired. I was ordered to guard
the wagon with our tents and baggage. After guard duty I
laid down my musket and bayonet and collapsed with the men.
We are sleeping five deep. Tom is nowhere around. I shouldn't
wonder if he's over with his nurse, Emma Dooley again. I
was surprised she marched with us and didn't remain with
the other nurses. She is one of a few who came. I heard her
pleading with one of the officers to be permitted to come along.

Tom took all my food rations yesterday on a game of
cards with not an ounce of remorse. I lay on my knapsack
and despite the pangs of hunger fell asleep within minutes
like a baby, waking in the morning wet from the overnight
shower.

August 28, 1862. Today, we gorged on blackberries as we moved eastward. We will pay the toll with upset bellies. The supplies are all gone and we're famished. Old man Lee wanted to draw the bluebellies into a fight. By early evening we saw the ravages of war as we came late to a battle already done. We were lucky. Our boys fared well with relatively few casualties beating back the Yankees. Tom disappeared, I assumed to Emma Dooley. I found his bayonet lying idly next to my knapsack. He's looking for trouble. I've heard talk we are heading for Jackson's right flank.

August 29, 1862. Today we marched into battle. The fighting was long and hard. Blood everywhere. Shattered raggedy bodies. Horses crushing soldiers as they buckled to the ground with their wounds. I thought it would never end. Many bullets whizzed past my ears. But none with my name. This time. So many of my friends dead. How can so much killing be just?

"Did Thomas Garnet get wounded in the fighting?" asked Raj.

"If you'd both just wait up, you'll see," I said.

The sun mocked us as it shone high in the blue sky. I hurried to fill my cartridge and cap box with ammunition. The bloody sight of men and horses scattered through the fields will haunt me forever. I was told to be a sharpshooter to cover the stream and prevent the Yankees filling their canteens. I saw Tom Garnet's young nurse Emma Dooley take her fill. I was glad she was one of ours. If she had been from the Union, I doubt I could have shot her. We advanced and I had to wade through the broken bodies of my fellow soldiers. We were exhausted, dying of thirst if not from a bullet. Tom Garnet is missing. I searched among the dead bodies but could not find him.

Aug. 30. 1862. Victory was sweeter than molasses. The Yankees have retreated and left us with their wounded. I saw Emma Dooley giving water to the prisoners. Any other would have stopped her, but I could not do that. I asked her if she'd seen Tom, but she turned away and wouldn't answer. I caught sight of General Longstreet and swung my hat high on my bayonet and shouted a triumphant hurrah.

Then I saw him. Tom Garnet.

He was dead. But not from a bullet. There he swung like a bee infested fruit. Tom Garnet, my friend, a Yankee spy. I can't believe it. My fellow soldiers came and took him after the final battle. He'd been seen dressed in one of the officer's uniforms again and talk was they'd found secret letters addressed to the Union in his knapsack. To think I believed his story that he was after the young nurse, Emma Dooley. Will she mourn like I do? I wrote a poem for him and buried it under cover of darkness buried it under the tree.

I got to my feet and leaned back against the bookshelf.

"Why would anyone volunteer to be a spy?" said Raj. "Wasn't it dangerous enough to be fighting?"

"The army generals made it sound exciting." I picked up Raj's book and thumbed through the pages. "I read that the company captain would call for volunteers for extra dangerous duty."

"Neat," said Danny.

"Yeah, who wouldn't be intrigued by a little extra adventure?" I agreed.

"Me," said Raj.

"Apart from you," I said. "Apparently these men were often very bright, clever men. Thomas Garnet didn't appear particularly smart."

"I guess you can't always judge someone by the way they look." Raj glanced at Danny with his thorny hair, shorts down to his ankles and Pokemon T-shirt with a chocolate stain on the front.

True.

"So he was a spy," I said. "There's the proof."

Danny got to his feet and handed me the sheets of parchment from the ground. Then he went over to the large bookshelf in the middle of the small room and took out a dusty, red book. "These are the records of enlistment. This book is for the Seventeenth Virginia Infantry Regiment." He leafed through the pages until he found what he was searching for. "And here is Thomas Garnet's name and where he signed."

There was a big X next to his name.

"Why didn't he sign his name?" wondered Raj aloud.

"An 'x' means he couldn't read or write. That was common in those days."

"So Thomas Garnet was hanged in your tree for being a spy and that's why he didn't want you to cut it down. It was that simple? That's the mystery?" Raj sounded disappointed.

"What was that simple?" Mom's voice cut through the air. In our excitement we hadn't heard her return. I slid the original documents behind my back. Danny's eyes darted from me to the wide-open, red door. In a flash he bent double and clutched his hand to his mouth.

"I think I'm going to throw up," he moaned. "Mom, can you take me to the bathroom?" He was pretty good at acting. His face appeared almost green.

"Sure, honey, come with me." Mom led Danny out of the room, and as soon as they'd disappeared, I quickly replaced the parchment in the filing cabinet and locked the red door just as Mom returned.

"I'm sorry, lads, but we'll have to head on out," she said. "I think Danny might be coming down with a bug. He was just sick to his stomach."

Now there's acting and there's acting.

On the drive back I pondered the information we had discovered. If Thomas Garnet had been a Union spy, then what was his problem? They'd won, hadn't they? Didn't he read the papers? Why couldn't his soul rest in peace? Was he ashamed of being a spy? It made no sense. And why was it important for me to see that torn piece of paper, and what did the red markings on the ticket mean? If Thomas Garnet was a *Union* soldier, why did he leave the Confederate flag for me next to the shape of a heart in the snow? We hadn't solved the puzzle, we'd simply found the four corners. We had the whole middle section to complete, and without a finished picture the solution was about as clear as pudding.

Chapter Twelve
Will the Real Spy Please Stand Up?

"Have you heard the news?" Raj came running up to me. "Alan Idle has been suspended."

A strange sickly feeling churned away in my stomach.

"They found the stolen goods in his locker," said Raj. "Can you believe that?"

"Did he admit to it?" I said.

"Mike Tucker said Alan denied everything. He said someone planted the gear. But then he would say that, wouldn't he? This is the best news, don't you think?"

I didn't know what to think. Sure, the prospect of life without Alan Idle was like Christmas arriving at Easter, but he was innocent of the theft. I'd seen Tiger Stone place the stolen stuff in Alan's locker. Tiger Stone was the real culprit. But with Alan gone, Raj could avoid further scar tissue and wouldn't need Tiger Stone's protection anymore. Two bullies gone in one swoop. So why wasn't I overjoyed?

The answer was simple. Alan Idle didn't do it, and I knew who did.

Raj punched me playfully in the arm. "Hey, cheer up. We're rid of the school's biggest bully, and we've solved the mystery of the ghost. We should go get ice cream after school to celebrate."

Whoopee.

Raj bounced along swinging his school bag, but I trailed behind. Martin Luther King Junior's words were still shouting on the sign outside the school. *The Time Is Always Right To Do What Is Right.*

In my heart, the right thing would be to tell the principal what I'd witnessed, but why should I help Alan Idle after what he'd done to Raj?

I turned my head away from the sign, ignoring the wise words and didn't see the cracked concrete in the sidewalk. I tripped and whacked my chin on the gravel. Boy, did it hurt.

That evening I called Raj and invited him over for a sleepover. When he arrived, I broke the news—we were going to hold a séance.

"What's a séance?" asked Danny as we congregated in our bedroom. It was after ten and Mom had just instructed us to turn out the lights so Danny could get some sleep.

"A séance is where we talk to spirits of the dead," I said.

"Count me out." Raj tunneled into his sleeping bag and pulled the top flap over his head.

"Don't be stupid. It'll be fun," I said. Although I had to admit, the idea of talking to spooks wasn't in my top ten of favorite activities.

"Why do we need to talk to Thomas Garnet?" asked Raj. "We know the deal. He was a spy, end of story."

"But that doesn't explain why he would be so angry. He was on the winning side. No, there has to be more to it. We need to communicate with him," I said. "First we have to make sure the room is in complete darkness."

Danny stood up and flicked the light switch.

"And we should pull down the blind, otherwise it won't be dark enough."

Raj climbed out of his sleeping bag and went over to the window. "Wow, look at the tree! Its branches are shaking like it's having a fit. I've never seen anything like it."

"There's our proof," I said. "That's the work of Thomas Garnet. He's dying for us to start."

Raj groaned. "So cheesy."

"Okay, you guys. Get ready to meet the deceased," I said.

We gathered on the floor between the two beds. "We should really be sitting around a table," I said, "but I think it's okay if we sit on the floor as long as our hands touch. We have to form a circle and not let it break."

"Why not?" asked Raj.

"I don't know," I said. "That's what it said on the 'how to have a séance' web site."

Danny slid his hand into my hand and curled his little fingers around mine.

I shook him off. "We don't have to actually hold hands. Our fingers just need to be touching."

"But I'm scared," he said. "It's too dark in here."

"Nothing's going to happen," I said. So I lied.

"If nothing's going to happen, why are we doing this?" asked Raj.

I glared at him and nodded my head toward Danny. We sat very still, squinting at each other's shapes in the blackness.

"Now what?" said Raj after a couple of minutes with nothing happening.

"I don't know," I said. "Maybe we should close our eyes."

We squeezed our lids shut, but after thirty seconds I peeked out only to see Danny and Raj both squinting too and giggling. "Come on you two, quit messing around. We have to do this seriously."

More waiting and silence. "Is there anybody there?" I asked finally.

Still nothing. I grabbed the closest book from under my bed and placed it in the middle of the circle between us and tried again. "Thomas Garnet, if you're there, knock three times on—" I turned on the light for a second and looked at the name of the book, "—*The Gas We Pass: The Story of Farts.*" We waited again.

Raj took a book from under Danny's bed and slid it over. "Try this one, *Spying at Bull Run.*"

The light went back off, and back in the darkness we waited again.

Then three loud bangs rapped at the door. If Raj had been a kangaroo he'd have won the Marsupial High Jump Olympics hands-down. I'd have come in a close second. A cold sweat washed over me as my heartbeat quickened.

Mom's voice broke the tension.

"No more talking, boys. Danny has to get some sleep," she hollered through the door.

"Okay, Mom," I said. We waited without talking to give Mom time to go downstairs.

"Well, that was a waste of time." I clambered up onto my bed.

Danny scrambled to his bed and burrowed under his blankets. Raj snuggled into the sleeping bag on the ground between us. There was a disgusting smell. Someone had cut one. I was about to ask who was the culprit when I noticed something strange happening. I tried to speak but the words backed up in my brain like the long line of yellow buses fleeing the school grounds at three in the afternoon. The pages of Danny's book were magically flipping.

"Can you see that?" whispered Raj in a quivering voice. He sat up in his sack, recoiling like an accordion. "Is the window open?" he asked nervously.

"Raj, it's the middle of winter, of course the window isn't open." My voice cracked. "It's stopped."

I switched on the light beside my bed and shimmied to the edge. "Pick it up and see which chapter it stopped at."

Raj reached out with the enthusiasm of stroking a rattlesnake.

"Well, which chapter is it?" I asked.

"Civil War Spies," said Raj. "And it has a whole page of old photos."

I groaned. "Okay, okay. We know you're a spy," I said, talking to the ceiling.

"But wait," said Raj. "This chapter is specifically about female spies. This page is a memoir written by a Union spy called Emma Dooley. There's a photo of parts of a note that has been torn up, and there's a photograph of her on the page but she's dressed up as a nurse. That's odd, and why do I know that name? Is that the new girl in sixth grade? The one with onion breath?"

"No. Emma Dooley was the nurse in the soldier's journal. The nurse Thomas Garnet was friendly with," I said.

I clambered off my bed, took the book from Raj, and in a whisper read aloud.

Before the battle, I had lived on a farm a few miles outside of Manassas. During the spring of eighteen-sixty-two, a slave, who had been issued a pass to go through Confederate lines three times a week to sell his produce, brought me a message from the Union. They knew my sympathies lay with the North and wanted to recruit me. The slave had rolled up the message in a piece of tin foil and hid it under his tongue. I willingly agreed to spy for the Union revealing details of many Confederate battalions' movements. To get close to a rebel regiment I disguised myself as a nurse pinning a red ribbon to my chest like the symbol of the Red Cross.

My eyes flicked down the page. *In case my secret letters were intercepted, I tore each note into four and sent them separately.*

"So they were both spies?" Raj stretched out in his bag. A wind whipped up and the light by my table flickered. I shivered.

"Unless Thomas Garnet's story was true," I said. "What if he *was* trying to impress her, and that's why he was wearing an officer's uniform, when all along she was the spy? When she thought she was about to be uncovered, she planted the note about the battalion's movements in Thomas Garnet's knapsack."

"Does it say that in the book?" asked Raj.

"No," I said, searching the page. "This seems to be just an extract. The story stops there."

"But why would she frame Thomas Garnet?" asked Raj.

Danny sat up on his bed. "Because she didn't want to be found out. If she was close to being discovered, maybe she needed to find an escape animal."

"You mean a scapegoat," I said. It was a rare moment for me to correct brain-box, and it sure felt good.

"So Thomas Garnet wasn't a spy after all?" said Raj.

"No, I don't think so. He was a rogue and a bad guy. He scared old Mrs. Snell to death. He stole from his best friend and was a terrible soldier. But he was hanged for something he didn't do. He wasn't a Union spy. He was a Confederate soldier. That's what the flag and the heart in the snow meant. He loved the Confederacy and he wanted to clear his family name. And if the tree is chopped down, his soul will be stuck in limbo forever."

"But even if that is the truth," said Raj, "you can't prove it. You have no witnesses."

At that moment the walls shook, the windows rattled, and the wind outside howled like a tormented wolf.

"Jake, has the heating gone off? It's freezing in here," said Raj.

But this had nothing to do with our oil burner. I dashed to the window. Our oak tree was shooting snow and icicles from its branches. I opened my eyes wide with terror.

Suddenly there was a scream followed by heavy thumping like an elephant plummeting down the stairs.

"It's Mom," I said. "He's killed Mom." I ran across the room and yanked open the door. Mom stood at the top of the stairs at the end of the hallway. She was not very dead.

"Jake," she screeched, turning and giving me an agonized look. "How many times have I told you not to leave stuff on the stairs? I tripped and dropped the whole basket of clean laundry. I could have broken my neck." She handed me a shoe.

"That's not mine," I said.

"I don't care whose it is. I just wish you could try and be more tidy," said Mom.

"Would you like us to help you pick up the clothes?" said Raj, appearing at my shoulder. Danny was close behind.

"No, that's okay, Raj, but thanks for offering. Good night boys," she said in a firm voice.

We returned to the bedroom. "Do you think that was the work of Thomas Garnet?" asked Raj.

"Yes, I do," I said. "He wants us to clear his name. It's very simple."

"And if we can't?" asked Danny from back under his sheets.

"Can't isn't an option," I said in a solemn voice. "We have to."

But I knew it was no good. We couldn't prove anything. No judge was going to believe a bunch of kids with a ghost story. And our only witness was a big old tree with attitude. We were doomed. There was nothing we could do, and with Thomas Garnet's track record, we'd better invest in some heavy duty shovels and start digging our graves.

Chapter Thirteen
The Time Is Right

As hard as I tried I could not get to sleep that night. I was scared if I closed my eyes I might wake up in the morning, dead. I waited until I could hear Danny's rhythmic breathing, then called over to Raj. It wasn't quite midnight.

"Are you awake?" I whispered.

"Yes," he said. "Do you think he's going to show himself tonight?"

"I don't know. But I have a question. If we did have proof, do you think we should try and clear Thomas Garnet's name?" I stared out into the darkness.

"Of course," said Raj without hesitation, "if he didn't do it."

"Raj, there's something I have to tell you. Alan Idle didn't steal the stuff at school."

"What?"

I could hear the rustle as Raj moved around in his bag.

"It was Tiger Stone," I said. "I saw him hide the gear in Alan Idle's locker."

There was a long silence.

"You have to tell the principal," Raj said eventually. "It's the right thing to do."

"I know," I said. "I was going to, but I wanted to tell you first."

"Thanks."

I waited for a proverb. It took five minutes. A long five minutes.

"If you sit on the bank of a river and wait," muttered Raj, "your enemy's corpse will soon float by."

That would be good.

After some time we fell asleep and woke up the next morning still breathing.

At the breakfast table, after piles of pancakes drenched in maple syrup, I suggested a game of basketball. The weather had warmed up and the snow was starting to melt, and we still had half an hour before we had to go to school.

"The snow has almost gone," I said. "I challenge you to a one-on-one."

"Can I play, too?" asked Danny. He was lost without Edward.

"Sure."

Outside, the oak tree stood by innocently as Raj slam dunked the first basket. I had my back to the road. I felt a pair of eyes watching me and spun around expecting to see the barrel of a gun or a bloodied saber, but there was nobody there. I couldn't bear it. Thomas Garnet was everywhere and nowhere.

Then I had a thought. "I'm just going inside to get something. Be right back."

I raced up the front steps and into the house and returned a few minutes later with a hefty book, a pencil and a pad of paper.

Danny continued to shoot hoops as Raj came over to join me on the front step.

"I've had an idea," I said in an excited tone. "I think I just found our proof."

"What are you talking about?" asked Raj, shoving his hands in his pockets.

I waved the text book in the air. "This is one of Danny's Civil War books, the one about the spies. This is our proof that Thomas Garnet couldn't have been a spy." I balanced the heavy book on my knee, opened it, and propped my pad on one side. "I'm going to make a list of all the clues." I scribbled on the paper. "Number one: the shadow of the noose."

"That was Thomas Garnet's way of telling us he was hanged," offered Raj.

"Correct. Number two: the Confederate flag and the heart." I shifted my butt on the step to get more comfortable. "Okay, that must have been him informing us he was fighting for the South."

"And clue number three?" asked Raj.

"That was the sketch on the back of the Manassas Battle-field Museum ticket." I continued to write as I explained the clues. "It was meant to be the ribbon worn by the nurses during the war. Emma Dooley was a nurse. I think Thomas Garnet was trying to point her out as our prime suspect."

"Were there any more clues?" Raj plonked himself down next to me on the cold step.

"Yes. The final clue was the torn piece of the letter that Thomas Garnet left. Until now, I could not work out why

Thomas Garnet would want us to have it. Unless it was important in proving his innocence."

A stray basketball came flying our way. Raj caught it and tossed it back to Danny. "What are you getting at?" he asked.

"Remember the soldier's journal, how he noted that he had to write the letter for Thomas Garnet?" I said.

"So?"

"Come on, Raj. Think about it. The enlistment records at the museum showed that Thomas Garnet had signed his name with an X. Don't you get it?"

Raj continued to look very puzzled. "Nope."

I laid my pad of paper on the step and flicked through the textbook. "Qualities for a spy," I read. "They were intelligent, resourceful, and had to send back letters to their own army. There's no way Thomas Garnet could have been a spy. Thomas Garnet couldn't write. He was illiterate. That's why he wanted us to connect Emma Dooley with the torn letter— he couldn't have written it. But Emma Dooley could have."

Danny ambled over dribbling the basketball. "You know the note you found, and the stuff that soldier wrote in his journal. Well, I read somewhere that during the Battle of Second Manassas General Pope didn't get good information about where Longstreet's army was. So that note from the nurse would have been pretty important. She must have really been close to being discovered to not send that note."

"Remind me again, Danny." I looked up from the step. "Who was on which side?"

Danny hurled the basketball toward the net. "Longstreet was a Confederate under General Robert E. Lee, and John Pope was a general for the Union under President Lincoln. If Emma Dooley had sent the note, maybe the Yankees would have changed their plan of attack."

"But she didn't send it. It was a perfect way to frame Thomas Garnet as a spy," I said.

"Do you think with proof that Thomas Garnet was illiterate we can get someone to clear his name?" asked Raj.

"I would think so. I'm just not sure who we would need to write to. We could ask Ms. Browne. She might know." I stood up and folded my list of evidence into four.

We *could* try and clear Thomas Garnet's name. But the question was, should we? He was not exactly a hero, but did he deserve to be hanged for something he didn't do?

At the first opportunity at school, I approached Ms. Browne and explained our predicament. Instead of laughing her head off at the mention of a ghost she was intrigued.

"This is absolutely fascinating, Jake," she said, flinging her fur scarf over her left shoulder. I tried not to stare at the dead raccoon wrapped around her neck. "Have you met this Thomas Garnet? Could I meet him, too? I have so much to ask him." Danny and Ms. Browne would get on so well.

"He doesn't exactly come to order," I said. "But you do think we could get a pardon?"

"It's certainly worth a try." She pulled open a drawer in her desk and extracted a sheet of paper. She scribbled down some details, her heavy metal bracelets clanging together like church bells as she wrote, and handed the notes to me. "Service records of any man or woman who has served in one of the forces are held by the National and State Archives in Richmond, Virginia. As state governors have the ability to grant pardons, I suggest you write to the Governor of Virginia at this address."

Thanking Ms. Browne, I ran outside to find Raj. Instead it was Tiger Stone I came across, hanging around behind one of the trailers. He was with his usual group of deadbeats. It was now or never. Pushing the image of Tiger Stone's brothers and the Skull gang armed with knives to the back of my mind, I took a deep breath and marched up to him.

"Tiger, I need to speak to you," I said, in a shaky voice. "It's about the stolen goods in Alan Idle's locker. I saw you stash them in there."

Tiger glanced at his two friends. "He's talking trash. Don't listen to him. He didn't see nothing."

"You're wrong, Tiger," I said. "I saw everything, and if you don't go to the principal then I will."

"I'm so scared." He let out a nervous giggle.

It was time to stand up to him. "If you don't own up, then I'm telling everything I saw, I swear."

"Did you steal the stuff?" said one of Tiger's sidekicks to Tiger.

"'Course I did," said Tiger, "But who's gonna prove it—that little jerk. He's bluffing. He's not gonna tell the principal 'cause that'll bring back Alan Idle." He swung around and positioned his face inches from mine. "Unless he likes to see his little friend getting beaten up, of course."

No, I didn't, but I knew the difference between right and wrong, and I couldn't stand by and see someone expelled for something he didn't do.

"He doesn't need to tell me." Principal Moon appeared around the corner. "I just heard it from the horse's mouth. Tiger Stone, you'd better come with me."

As the days passed we waited to hear back from the governor. But we got nothing in the mail the next day, nor the day after that, nor the day after that. Our oak went quiet and so did Thomas Garnet. I guessed he was waiting, too.

Now if this were a soppy movie, when Alan Idle returned to Longstreet Middle School, he'd be so grateful that we had helped him out he'd be a reformed kid and we'd be the best of friends forever. But as I told you before, this is real. This is my life.

We were outside the school getting ready to walk home reading the school's new message on the sign outside, a quote by Ralph Waldo Emerson, *Always Do What You Are Afraid To Do,* when we spotted Alan Idle heading our way.

"Hey, butt-face," he said when he saw Raj. "Did ya miss me?" He came close and jabbed Raj in the shoulder.

It was quite clear Alan Idle was still a bully and a jerk, and that wasn't going to change anytime soon. But what Alan didn't know was that Raj had taken my advice. On the news of Alan Idle's imminent return, he had done what any other self-respecting pre-teen would do. He'd enrolled in a crash course of Karate classes. Raj pulled up both his arms into a cross in front of his chest and chopped at the air. He was very fast and his eyes flashed with his new-found courage and determination. He was not one to be messed with. "Be First at the Feast, and Last at the Fight," he said to Alan.

Alan gave him a blank stare then did something he'd never done before. He walked away. He realized we were not going to take it anymore. He didn't scare us, and it felt fantastic.

Three weeks later, I was doing homework in my room when Mom yelled up the stairs. "Jake, phone."

I headed downstairs into the kitchen and picked up the phone from the counter where Mom had left it. "Hello," I said. "Yes, this is Jake Salmon. Yes, Sue Garnet is my mom. Really. Tight. Sure. Thanks." I replaced the receiver.

"Who was that?" asked Mom.

"That was Mr. Shively," I said, grinning.

"And who's Mr. Shively?" asked Mom. "What have you been up to?" She pulled out a chair to join Dad at the kitchen table. Dad was building a model marble run out of toothpicks for Danny.

"Mr. Shively works in the State Archives of Virginia. He received my letter I sent to the governor about Thomas Garnet, our ghost—"

Mom rolled her eyes. "Please tell me you're kidding! You didn't write to the governor about your silly ghost."

"He's not a silly ghost. And Ms. Browne from school told me to write to him."

Mom slapped her hand on the kitchen table. "You involved your teacher, too. Oh, Jake."

"No wait. I have some good news—"

Mom held up her hand as she stood up and walked over to the kitchen sink. "I don't want to hear it," she said with her back to me.

"Let him finish," said Dad. "Go on, Jake, tell us your news. In fact, why don't you tell us the whole story?"

I held the back of the chair to steady myself, pausing for dramatic effect. "You know our ghost is called Thomas Garnet and he was a Confederate soldier hanged as a Union spy on the tree in our front yard?"

Dad rubbed the stubble on his chin. "I didn't know that, but go on."

"Well, ghosts always haunt for a reason, and Thomas Garnet needed someone, me, to help him clear his name." I waited for the praise and gasps of astonishment. When none came, I continued. "First I saw the shadow of the noose on my closet door. To begin with I thought I was imagining it—" Now everyone nodded. I ignored them. "—but then I found the Confederate flag under the tree and the heart drawn in the snow." Mom and Dad stopped nodding as their faces crinkled in confusion. Mom returned to the washing-up, but Danny hopped up and down the kitchen floor in excitement. He knew what was coming. "This was Thomas Garnet's way of making it clear that he was a Confederate soldier. But at this point, even though we realized he wasn't the spy, we had no clue who the real spy was, until—" I paused again for effect, "I recognized the sketch Thomas Garnet had scribbled on the back of a Manassas Battle Field ticket stub. It was a drawing of the ribbons worn by the nurses during the war. He was telling us the spy was a nurse."

"Yeh," said Mom, turning around from the dishes and punching the air. She was being sarcastic. Dad gave her a grave look and lowered his chin, a sign for me to go on.

"The only thing we had to do now, and this was the hardest part, was to find some proof. That was when I remembered what we'd read about how to be a spy. We already knew that Thomas Garnet was illiterate."

Dad raised his eyebrows.

"Trust me on this, Dad. So that was all the proof we needed. He couldn't have written the spy notes, but Emma Dooley, the nurse who he'd been hanging around with, could have. So I wrote to the governor and got Thomas Garnet a pardon. And Mom, this is the best bit."

A faint smile crept onto her face.

"The Governor said that Thomas Garnet was a distant relative of Grandma Garnet's. Can you believe that?"

Danny's eyes flashed in excitement. "I'm going to write a family tree. I'll start with Thomas Garnet. Do you think we could get him to appear—just one more time, so that I could ask him about his family?"

"No, Danny, definitely not," Mom said with determination. "We've had more than enough of that Thomas Garnet.

You can go to a genealogy website like any normal human being where they'll help you trace your ancestry. It's time to say goodbye to our nighttime visitor."

For once I agreed with Mom. No more sleepless nights. No more nighttime hauntings. Thomas Garnet could finally rest, and I could plan for my thirteenth birthday. The ice cream was definitely on me. As Raj would say, "One ghost in the house is one ghost too many."

Okay, I made that one up.

Educational Resources

The Battles of Manassas, Virginia

Two battles took place around the stream Bull Run, situated near the small Virginia town of Manassas Junction.

The **First Battle of Bull Run** (or the Battle of First Manassas, as it was called by the Confederate army) took place on July 21, 1861. This one-day battle was considered the first major battle of the Civil War. Many in Washington did not expect the war to last very long and, thinking this would be their only opportunity to see a battle, rode out to watch the spectacle like an afternoon's entertainment. However, the onlookers were soon sent running for their lives when a horrendous battle ensued and the Union army came streaming back through the crowd in defeat. The Confederates were under the command of Generals Joseph E. Johnston and Pierre G. T. Beauregard while the Union army was led by Brigadier General Irvin McDowell. Although early in the day the Union army had the upper hand and the Confederates were outnumbered, the timely arrival of Johnston's reinforcements turned the tide of battle. By late afternoon the Union army was retreating in confusion. Although the rebel army now had command of the battle, they were too inexperienced and exhausted to continue a pursuit and the battle ended with almost five thousand casualties. It was at this battle that Confederate Brigadier General Thomas J. Jackson earned his nickname, "Stonewall" Jackson, for his solid stand on Henry Hill.

The **Battle of Second Bull Run** (or the Battle of Second Manassas, as it was called by the Confederate army) took place the following year on August 28–30, 1862, with General Robert E. Lee commanding the Army of Northern Virginia for the Confederates and Union Major General John Pope his adversary. It began on the evening of August 28 when General Jackson ordered an attack against a Federal column that was marching across his front on the Warrenton Turnpike. The intense fight lasted a few hours until dark with no winner but significant losses of life. The next day, August 29, Pope launched multiple attacks against Jackson's position along an unfinished railroad. Even though Jackson warded off each attack, heavy casualties resulted, once again, on both sides. During the battle, Major General James Longstreet moved his thirty thousand men into position opposite Pope's left flank. The following day, August 30, Pope renewed his attack against Jackson, but a massive counterattack by Longstreet's forces devastated the Union left and Pope was forced to retreat. On the back of this Confederate victory, on August 31, General Lee ordered his army to pursue. It is believed there were more than twenty thousand casualties in this decisive battle.

Reading Group
Discussion Questions

1. In the food chain Jake describes himself and Raj as grass-hoppers, Tiger Stone a deadly hawk, and Alan Idle the field mouse. Discuss?

2. Raj says your enemy's enemy is therefore your friend. Do you agree?

3. During the Civil War many captured women spies were given a quick reprimand and sent back out, often to continue spying. Why was this, and how do you think this has changed today?

4. What did Martin Luther King, Junior, mean by his statement, *The Time Is Always Right To Do What Is Right*, and how does this relate to Jake and Raj's confrontation with Alan Idle and Tiger Stone?

5. What does the proverb *You can keep ten yards from a horse, and a hundred yards from an elephant, but the distance you should keep from a wicked man cannot be measured* mean?

6. When does Jake come to the conclusion that the noises he has been hearing are coming from a ghost? What evidence does he find, and would you have come to the same conclusion?

7. Why is the old oak in the front yard referred to as a "witness tree"?

8. What qualifications make a great spy?

9. How has espionage changed since the 1800s?

10. What is Bletchley Park, and what role did it play in World War Two?

11. How did the roles of female spies differ from male spies?

Author's Note
Women Spies in the Civil War

Did you know?

- Women spies used many everyday items to hide their secret messages and important information, including the cases of watches, false-bottom trays, double bottom dishes, hollowed-out shoe soles and cut-out books.

- Sometimes spies would use a pin to prick the letters of words printed in books to spell out secret messages and pass the books back and forth to captured soldiers in prisons.

- It is believed that up to one thousand women disguised themselves as men to serve as soldiers in the Civil War, and many of these double disguised themselves back as women to spy for their army.

Here are some examples of Female Civil War Spies both Union and Confederate:

· **Sarah Emma Edmonds**, a spy for the Union army, first disguised herself as a man named Franklin Thompson, in order to enlist in the Michigan volunteer infantry, then changed her gender *and* race by dressing in slave clothing, cutting her hair short and wearing a black wig, and smearing silver nitrate into her skin to dye it black. In her disguise as a male African-American slave she was able to gain important information from the Confederate camps and take it back to the Union army. After she was exposed as a spy, she was released and became a nurse for the Union.

Harriet Tubman, although more famous for her involvement in the Underground Railroad, also served as a Union spy while in the U.S. Army in South Carolina. She organized scouts and spies among the African-American men in the area, encouraging slaves to flee from their owners and join the African-American soldiers for the Union. Under the command of Colonel James Montgomery, a defender of the rights of the anti-slavery settlers, Tubman was one of the few women to actually lead a raid, which destroyed bridges and railroads and freed hundreds of African-American slaves.

Elizabeth Van Lew, nicknamed by her neighbors Mad Lizzie or Crazy Bet, was an abolitionist educated in a Quaker school in Philadelphia. Miss Van Lew persuaded her mother in Richmond to free the family slaves, then brought food and clothing to Union prisoners held at the Confederate Libby Prison in Richmond. In her baskets of food she would smuggle information back and forth between the captured Union soldiers and the Federal army, even passing secret information to General Grant. She invented her own secret code, which she kept hidden in the case of her watch. When milk was poured onto the message the code would appear.

Mary Elizabeth Bowser, a former slave of the Bowser family, was sent to Philadelphia to be educated. Then Elizabeth Van Lew had Mary Elizabeth hired as a maid in the home of Jefferson Davis in order to act as a Union spy.

Dr. Mary Walker, a nurse and spy for the Union, was awarded the Congressional Medal of Honor for her Civil War service. She liked to wear pants—bloomers as they were then called (until the late 1800s when the bicycle was invented it was pretty unusual for a woman to wear pants)—and became the first woman to hold a Congressional Medal of Honor.

Pauline Cushman (real name Harriet Wood) started out as an actress on the stage before becoming a double agent for the Union army. However, she was captured with secret papers by the Rebels, tried, and condemned to hang. Three days before she was to go to the gallows, she was rescued by the Union army. Her gravestone in San Francisco National Cemetery states simply: Pauline C. Fryer, Union Spy

Belle Boyd, known as La Belle Rebelle, became a spy when she was seventeen, passing information about the Union activities to Stonewall Jackson. She was captured, imprisoned and released many times. She was brave and courageous, rode through the nighttime with cipher messages, sneaked around in rooms eavesdropping on Union army meetings, and could shoot straight and fast. She was very feminine and instead of trying to disappear into the background like other female spies, she did the opposite. She was a chatterbox, liked to dance and flirt with both Southern and Northern soldiers, and although she was imprisoned a number of times, when she was captured she used her feminine wiles to look sad and distraught and gain the sympathy of the Federal commanders who would then release her to spy again. She even married a

Union naval officer who helped her escape capture. After the war, Belle became an actress and on the stage recounted her many Civil War escapades.

Antonia Ford from Fairfax, Virginia, was a Confederate spy who also ended up marrying the Union major who guarded her after she was arrested. Antonia's brother served under General J. E. B. Stuart, and Antonia provided Stuart with information on Federal troop activities. When Antonia was captured as a Confederate spy she was imprisoned in Old Capitol Prison in Washington, D.C.—this site is now occupied by the Supreme Court. Her name has been linked with possibly assisting the Confederate scout Pvt. John Singleton Mosby in planning the Fairfax Courthouse raid.

Rose O'Neal Greenhow, the Rebel Rose, was in charge of a whole ring of spies providing the Confederates with the timetable for the Union army's movements towards Manassas in 1861. When she was arrested at her home by Allan Pinkerton, head of the detective agency and the Federal government's secret service, she quickly signaled to other members of her spy ring with a raised handkerchief, then chewed up and swallowed the important message she was carrying. In her home, under arrest, she managed to conceal her pistol, and later when imprisoned in the Old Capitol Prison in Washington, D.C., with her daughter Rose, she carried on collecting and dispatching key information to the Confederate army.

Nancy Hart was a Confederate sympathizer and her mother was first cousin to the future president, Andrew

Johnson. When Nancy was eighteen she led a raid against the Union army, and was captured by Union soldiers. But she tricked one of her captors and used his own gun to kill him before escaping.

Laura Ratcliffe lived in the Frying Pan area of Fairfax County, Virginia. Her home was occasionally used as a head-quarters for Pvt. John Singleton Mosby (the Confederate scout). Laura found out about a plot to capture Mosby and informed him so he could escape. Later, she helped Mosby by hiding a cache of captured Federal dollars. She would send him secret messages which she hid under a rock near her home.

The sisters **Ginnie and Lottie Moon** were both Confederate sympathizers. Lottie carried messages and dispatches for the South disguising herself as an old woman, and Ginnie passed messages to the Knights of the Golden Circle* in Ohio. Although Ginnie came under suspicion, she boldly stood up for herself, brandishing her Colt revolver when questioned about her movements by a Union soldier. The soldier hesitated long enough to give Ginnie time to swallow her most informative dispatches she was carrying. She was eventually arrested carrying morphine, opium and camphor (for medicinal purposes). When her sister, Lottie, came in disguise to try to gain her release, she was also arrested. Eventually the two sisters were released without charges and ordered out of the Union area.

---

*   The Knights of the Golden Circle was a secret society of Southern sympathizers founded by George W. L. Bickley with branches across both the Northern and Southern states. On their lapels the society members wore the head of Liberty cut from a copper penny, and because of that their enemies called them Copperheads after the poisonous snake.

Places to Visit

For further information and a real sense of what it was like to live during the Civil War, plan a visit to one of the Battlefield Museums along the East Coast, and while you're over this way, make sure you visit the International Spy Museum in D.C.

International Spy Museum
800 F Street NW
Washington, DC 20004
866-SPYMUSEUM
http://www.spymuseum.org

Manassas National Battlefield Park
12521 Lee Highway
Manassas, VA 20109
703-361-1339
http://www.nps.gov/mana

The Manassas Museum
9101 Prince William St.
Manassas,VA 20110
703-368-1873
http://www.manassasmuseum.org

Antietam National Battlefield
5831 Dunker Church Road
Sharpsburg, MD 21782
301-432-5124
http://www.nps.gov/anti/

The Author

K.E.M. Johnston was born in Gibraltar, studied Business and International Marketing in the UK, speaks French and German, and worked in advertising and public relations in London's Covent Garden before moving to the US. She is widely published in children's, parent and business magazines, and when not working on her current novel, tutors a group of sixth-grade students in Creative Writing.

Ms. Johnston now lives in suburban Northern Virginia, on the outskirts of Washington, D.C., and a few miles from historic Manassas, the location for *The Witness Tree and the Shadow of the Noose*, with her British husband and three American sons who have not the slightest trace of a British accent.

Of Related Interest

HOUSE OF SPIES
Danger in Civil War Washington
Margaret Whitman Blair

Rob and Sarah are Civil War reenactors swept back to 1861 through the medium of Civil War photography. They arrive in Washington, D.C., just after the battle of Manassas, when people in the capital are reeling from the shock of Confederate victory. After Rob and Sarah were arrested as enemy spies, Rob's younger brother Jamie time-travels to the past to try to rescue them. The three young people must sort out whom to trust—and whom not to trust—in the topsy-turvy world of civil war espionage.

ISBN 978-1-57249-161-8 • Paperback $8.95

REBEL HART
Edith Morris Hemingway and Jacqueline Cosgrove Shields

A farm girl from the mountains of what was to become the state of West Virginia, 16-year-old Nancy Hart left home to join the Moccasin Rangers, a group of Rebel raiders who struck Federal army encampments quickly and then returned to hiding in the caves and hills they knew so well. Rumored to be a Rebel guide and spy, warrants circulated the area for her capture. Shunned by her family, twice captured by the enemy and with a price on her head, Nancy soon found herself in a day-to-day struggle for survival.

ISBN 978-1-57249-186-1 • Paperback $8.95

YANKEE SPY
A Union Girl in Richmond during the Peninsular Campaign
Maureen Stack Sappéy

Disillusioned with the social life that occupies her sister Julia and her friends, Louisa Holmes determines that she will somehow contribute to the success of General George C. McClellan and the Army of the Potomac as they fight their way toward the Confederate capital. One night, a doctor appears at her door with the urgent request that she travel to Richmond, Virginia, to deliver a pocket watch to an officer serving directly under President Jefferson Davis. How can a Union patriot like Louisa approach Major Robert Petrie with any hope of succeeding in her mission? How will a Confederate officer receive her?

ISBN 978-1-57249-135-9 • Paperback $5.99

WHITE MANE PUBLISHING CO., INC.

To Request a Catalog Please Write to:

WHITE MANE PUBLISHING COMPANY, INC.

P.O. Box 708 • Shippensburg, PA 17257

e-mail: marketing@whitemane.com

Breinigsville, PA USA
14 December 2009
229171BV00002B/1/P